Fierce Competition
A Novella

Fierce Competition
© 2012 Mark A. Roeder

Cover Photo Credit: Ron Chapple on Dreamstime.com.

Cover Design: Ken Clark

ISBN-13: 978-1475267839

ISBN-10: 1475267835

All Rights Reserved

Printed in the United States of America

Acknowledgements

I'd like to thank Robbie Ellis-Cantwell, Ken Clark, and James Adkinson for all the work they put in proofreading this book. Without their dedication my grammatical ineptitude would be on display for all to see.

Dedication

This book is dedicated to camp counselors everywhere. I was one of you for many years. I know the rewards, the hard work, and the exhaustion that go with the job.

Chapter One—I Spot the Most Beautiful Boy in the Universe and Meet My Archenemy

Camp Neeswaugee—Northern Indiana
First Day of Camp—August 9, 2010
Curtis

I just stared the first time I set eyes on Cody. In a word he was HOT! I glimpsed him only for a few moments as he walked down the hill with a couple of other boys, but his image was burned into my mind. Cody had medium-blond hair that was kind of long and fell down into his sexy emerald eyes. He was wearing only a bright-blue swimsuit, flip-flops, and a towel around his neck. He had really nice muscles and even a six-pack. Yum! I determined right then and there I *had* to get to know him. Perhaps camp wouldn't be a colossal waste of time after all.

"Curtis."

"Huh?"

"Take this," my Uncle Logan said as he pushed my backpack into my hands. I'd completely forgotten about my uncle for a few moments. Everything had gone out of my mind when I spotted Cody.

Logan grinned at me. He knew I'd been checking out Cody.

"Shut up," I said.

"I didn't say anything."

"You would have if I hadn't told you to shut up."

"Yeah, you're right."

Logan grabbed my other bag, and we walked toward my cabin.

"Please don't embarrass me," I said.

"Me?"

I turned around and gave him the stare of death.

"I'll try to control myself."

We walked down the hill and then up the steps of Cabin 34. I was excited. I was thirteen, but I'd never been to camp before. It was only for two weeks, but it was a chance to get away and live with other guys my own age. The six-week session at Camp Neeswaugee was for kids 9-11, but the two-week session was for kids 13-17. Uncle Logan told me the campers were split up by age, so everyone in my cabin would be either thirteen or fourteen.

I had come to have fun, but now I had another goal. I was determined to see just how far I could get with the hottie I'd spotted only moments before. Maybe by the end of the two-week session we might even make out. Mmm.

My counselor, Mr. Brubaker, introduced himself and led us into the cabin. Mr. Brubaker was about eighteen or nineteen. He was a little short, but built. He looked like a wrestler.

"Guys, this is Curtis," Mr. Brubaker said as we walked past his room and into the main area of the cabin.

There were eight other guys my own age standing around or unpacking. They looked like guys I could get along with. I tossed my backpack up onto the last available top bunk, claiming it as my own.

"This was my cabin when I was a counselor," Logan said, pointing up to the cabin plaques.

Large plaques ringed the top of the walls. Each had a nickname for the cabin, a cabin photo, and the names of the counselor and all the campers. The name Lincoln was on eleven of them.

"So you're Captain Lincoln," Mr. Brubaker said. "I've been staring at your name on those plaques all summer long.

"Yeah, I was in Division 4 for twelve years. My first summer I was a junior counselor. Later, I became the Division Commander of Division 6 and then the Indian-crafts director.

"Lads of Lincoln?" I asked, reading one of the cabin nicknames. "How lame is that?"

"My boys came up with that. They thought it was cool," Logan said.

"So you had all the rejects, huh?"

"You have everything, right? Underwear, socks..."

I glared at Logan. I knew he was trying to embarrass me.

"Isn't it time for you to drive back home now?" I asked.

"Okay! Okay! I'm going! Give me a hug."

I squirmed in Logan's grasp and pretended not to like it, but actually I did like it when he hugged me. I liked it a lot.

"I'll see you in two weeks," Logan said. He looked as if he wanted to muss my hair, but he didn't. That was one advantage to having it spiked. My hair was muss-proof.

Logan departed. One of the other boys walked over to me.

"Parents are so embarrassing, aren't they?" he said. "My name's Kirk."

"Curtis. He's my uncle, but he's as bad as a parent, and he actually enjoys embarrassing me. He is evil."

Kirk laughed.

"It's really cool he was a counselor for years and years. I don't know if I'd like the six-week camp. Two weeks is too long to be away from my computer and my cell. I'm already having text withdrawal."

"I'm going to die without my Wii," I said. "I tried to slip my cell phone past my uncle, but I got busted. That's one drawback of living with a former camp counselor. He knows all the tricks."

"I bet we can get a few things past our counselor," Kirk said quietly so Mr. Brubaker couldn't hear. "I bet he was a jock in high school. He's probably all muscles and no brains."

I laughed. I liked Kirk. I liked anyone who ragged on jocks.

"Jocks can't have brains. If they did, they wouldn't be jocks. No one with any sense would torture themselves with a football practice or strain their guts out lifting weights or run when nothing is chasing them."

Kirk laughed, and so did a couple of the other boys.

"I hate running unless I'm playing soccer with some friends," Kirk said. "I just play for fun. I'd never be on an official team."

"I don't run unless someone *much* bigger than me is going to kick my butt. If they're only a little bigger, I don't run. I'd rather fight than run."

Kirk laughed again.

"Let's go check this place out," Kirk said. "Come on, guys!"

Our whole cabin went out to explore. There were about thirty cabins, all identical to ours, up on a hill. There were three big shower houses with restrooms. Plus, there were other buildings. Down the hill were soccer fields, and beyond the fields was the girls' area. Across the road to the west was the Academy, and at the eastern end of the soccer fields was the main headquarters for the camp, the dining hall, and the smaller buildings for arts and crafts and other classes. There was even a library and a nature museum.

At lunch, Mr. Brubaker took us to the dining hall. The serving line was a lot like that at school, and we even had the same plastic lunch trays. The food seemed a lot better. There were individual pizzas and a great cherry-crumb dessert. There was a salad bar with pudding. There were also drink dispensers with milk, orange, grape, and cranberry juice and punch.

The main feature of the dining hall was Cody. I maneuvered my cabin into sitting next to his table so I would have a good view of him. He was so hot! His hard muscles made me breathe funny, but it was his face and hair that really got to me. He wasn't just cute. A lot of boys were cute. Cody was *way* cute! The way his hair fell down over his emerald eyes made me want to grab him, hug him, and kiss him on the lips. I blushed just thinking about it.

I didn't know Cody's name until one of the boys in his cabin called it out. The name fit him perfectly. He just looked like a Cody. I learned another name while I was sitting there and one that I'd quickly come to loathe: Elijah. He was sitting at another of the round tables near Cody, and he kept checking him out. He was being sly, but I knew exactly what he was doing. He was checking out my future boyfriend! I glared at him, but he didn't notice me. I hated to waste a good glare.

On the way out of the dining hall I "accidently" bumped into Elijah. He was checking out Cody's backside as he walked in front of us, and I didn't like it.

"Sorry," I said, making it clear with my tone of voice that I wasn't sorry at all. Elijah needed to keep his eyes off Cody. Cody was going to be mine!

"You don't like that kid very much do you?" Kirk asked as we split off from the group. Most of the cabin was heading up the hill, but we cut off to the left by unspoken agreement.

"Nope."

"Do you even know him?" Kirk asked, grinning.

"No, but I hate him."

"Why?" Kirk laughed.

I gave Kirk a sideways glance. I thought of making up some lame excuse or just a smart-alecky comment, but this was a two-week camp, and I had decided before I arrived to be completely myself here. If there was trouble, it wouldn't last long.

"Did you see that blond boy sitting at the table next to us? The really cute one who looks like a skater?"

Kirk eyed me suspiciously as I described Cody as cute.

"Yeah."

"That kid I bumped into accidentally-on-purpose, Elijah, was checking him out."

"You mean he's a homo?"

"Yeah."

"I guess we'd better be careful bending over to pick up the soap in the showers, then," Kirk said and laughed.

"I don't hate him because he's a homo," I said.

"What don't you like about him?"

"He's after the same boy I am."

Kirk stopped and looked at me without saying a word for a few moments.

"You're gay?"

"Yeah, so if you have a problem with that, then say whatever you have to say to me right now."

I crossed my arms and slipped into menacing mode.

"Wow. I never would have guessed. We only have one openly gay kid in my class, and he's really girly. He squeals if someone messes with his hair, and when he talks, he flails his hands around everywhere. You're nothing like him."

"There are all kinds of gay guys, Kirk, but you haven't told me if you have a problem with the fact that I'm gay."

"I don't have a problem with it. I'm not gay, but if you are...so what? I'll admit, it freaks me out just a little, but you're cool. Besides, you look like you're going to kick my butt if I say I have a problem with it."

I smiled, uncrossed my arms, and dropped out of menacing mode.

"No, but guys think twice before they attack if they think I'm a bad boy. Well, I *am* a bad boy, but my menacing look is a good defense."

"You've got to teach me how to do that. You were scary. Have guys attacked you?"

"Yeah."

"I hate bullies. This bigger kid used to push me around in grade school. I finally got tired of it and kicked him where it counts."

I laughed.

"What happened then?"

"He told on me. When my teacher asked me about it, I played innocent. She believed me, or pretended she did. She knew he was a bully, and I think she secretly approved."

"Nice. What did the bully do?"

"He came strutting up to me the next day, but instead of backing away, I walked toward him. He got this scared look on his face and then pretended he was walking over to the slide. I think he thought I was going to kick him in the same place again... and that's exactly what I was going to do."

Kirk nodded his approval.

"So, do you tell everyone you're gay?" Kirk asked.

"Only when it matters."

"Does your uncle know?"

"Yes."

"He's cool with it? You guys seem close."

"Yeah, he's cool with it, and we're pretty close now. He's gay, too.

"Really?"

"Yeah. He has a boyfriend."

"Wow. Hey, I'm sorry about the homo comment earlier and what I said about not bending over in the showers. I didn't really mean anything by it."

"Apology accepted. I think a lot of guys don't mean anything by it when they say stuff like that, but some do. That doesn't bother me as much as when someone says, 'That's so gay!' I feel like they're putting me down even though they aren't talking about me. Well, they are talking about me in a way. I *am* gay."

"Oh." Kirk looked uncomfortable. "I've said that before. I never thought it could hurt someone's feelings. I guess I just wasn't thinking."

"It doesn't bother me as much as it did when I was younger, but I still don't like it."

"Well, I will try never to say it again. You can remind me if I slip up."

"Deal."

"So, you like the skater-boy, huh?"

I liked the teasing tone to Kirk's voice. We walked up into the small wood-frame cabins where classes were held. There were also two real-log cabins.

"Yeah, his name is Cody, and he's so cute."

Kirk laughed.

"What?"

"I've just never heard a boy talk about another boy like that."

"That's only because you've never been fortunate enough to hang out with a homo before."

"Hey! Why do you get to say homo and I don't?"

"Because I am one! Have a problem with that?"

Kirk looked at me in wonder.

"You're not like I thought a gay guy would be like at all. You're so...bold."

"I'm bold, period. You've got to stop thinking all gay boys are alike. We're not. I don't have to act a certain way because I like boys. I'm just me, and I happen to be into guys instead of girls."

"It's so hard with girls!" Kirk said. "I get so nervous asking one out that I just about puke, and then I never know what she's thinking. Does she want me to kiss her, or is she going to slap my face? I usually end up doing a bunch of crap that I don't want to do when I'm out with a girl."

"Because you want to please her so she'll kiss you, right?"

"Mostly, except I usually don't get to kiss. It's kind of like buying a ticket to a movie and not getting to watch it."

I laughed.

"Yeah, you're a straight boy for sure. You are controlled by girls. I don't have that problem. Their tricks don't work on me. It's like having a superpower."

"I bet you love that."

"Why?"

"Well, if you have a superpower, then you probably get tights and a cape with that, right? You guys love to dress up, don't you?"

"Jerk."

Kirk laughed.

"*Homo*!" Kirk coughed into his fist. I liked how he teased me.

We walked on up the hill into the scouting area. Camp Neeswaugee was really big.

"What are you going to do to that kid, Elijah, if he keeps going after your boy?"

"I don't know yet. I'll come up with something suitably evil."

"I bet you will."

"Maybe I can stick him in a box and mail him home?"

"That would take way too much postage," Kirk said.

"True, and I only have $15. I have that money set aside for chocolate bars and soft drinks."

"How do you know he's interested in Cody, anyway?"

"I can tell by the way he looks at him. He wants him *bad*."

"Just like you."

"Yep."

"Um, how do you know Cody is gay, or do you know if he is or not? He doesn't look gay, but then neither do you."

"I don't know. I'm just hoping."

"What if he's not?"

"Then I'm writing a musical about losing the love of my life!"

"You homos are dramatic, aren't you?"

"I like to live life big! Hey! I didn't say you could use the word homo!"

"I'm allowed. My best friend at camp is gay, so I can say homo all I want."

"You know another gay kid here?"

Kirk rolled his eyes. "You gay boys aren't too smart, are you?"

"Hey!"

"I was talking about you."

"Oh!" I grinned. "Thanks!"

"Hey, I was just thinking," Kirk said.

"Isn't that difficult for you straight boys?"

"Funny! As I was saying, I was just thinking if Cody isn't gay, there's got to be other gay boys here. You and Elijah can't be the only ones. Maybe you can find another boy you like."

"Yeah, but it's hard to tell who is and who isn't gay. You can't go by the way a guy looks or acts. There is this boy, Jesse, at my school. If you met him you'd swear he's gay, but he's not."

"Then there's you. Before you told me about you, I would have sworn you weren't gay, but you are."

"Exactly. Unless a guy is out, it can be *really* hard to tell."

"I figured you guys could just tell by looking at each other."

"You're just full of misinformation, aren't you?"

"Well, pardon me, gay boy. We didn't study queer in school."

I laughed. "I like you."

"I like you, too. There is the added bonus that we won't like the same girl, because you don't like girls at all."

"Oh, I like girls. Girls are cool. I just don't *like* like them."

Kirk grinned and shook his head.

"I'm going to have a great report for school this year—*'How I Spent My Summer Studying a Homo'*."

"Funny."

We headed back toward our cabin.

"Hey," Kirk said. "Are you going to let the other guys know you're gay, or do we keep this a secret?"

"I'm not going to walk in and announce it, but I'm not keeping it a secret. You can say anything to me you want when they're around. They'll catch on."

"What if some of them have a problem with it?"

"Then I'll give them my bad-boy stare."

"That should work," Kirk said, then laughed. "You know, some of the guys are kind of scared of you."

"Me?"

"Yeah, that collar you wear makes you look dangerous."

"This?" I asked, grasping the black studded collar I wore around my neck. "If this scares them, they should see how I dress at home..." I laughed evilly, and Kirk grinned.

Chapter Two—Cody Likes Boys, Too!

Tuesday, August 10, 2010

I heard the first whispered rumors on the archery range just after lunch. During Indian crafts I eavesdropped on some girls who were talking in hushed voices about Cody. One of them was telling her friends that another friend, Mandy, had asked Cody to the dance on Friday night. Cody had told her he'd love to dance with her, but he wasn't used to dancing, because *he didn't go out with girls.*

I leaned a little closer under the guise of focusing on the shield I was painting red, black, and yellow.

"You mean...?" one of the girls asked.

"He's gay!"

"Yes!" I said, far too loudly and pumped my fist.

I looked around quickly when I realized what I'd done.

"This shield is coming out perfect!" I said.

Kirk, who was working not far away on a beaded bracelet for some girl he was crushing on, shoved his fist in his mouth trying not to laugh out loud at my outburst. It took several seconds for him to get himself under control.

"Yeah, that's...a great-looking shield, Curtis," he said. It was a nice try, but he was still trying not to laugh.

One of the girls, a cute blonde, was watching me. I had the feeling she didn't fall for my ruse, and Kirk was sure no help. I wasn't concerned with hiding the fact I was gay, but I didn't want everyone to know I had it bad for Cody.

My mind reeled as I sat there painting the horse on my shield. I couldn't believe it. Cody liked boys, too! That's what I'd hoped and dreamed since the moment I'd laid eyes on him. I'd operated as if he was gay, but I had no clue until now. Cody was absolutely, positively gay!

After class, Kirk walked with me down the hill toward main headquarters. He had a soccer class next, and I had wrestling. As soon as we were away from everyone else he turned to me.

"Yes!" he said, pumping his fist. I thought he was going to bust a gut laughing.

"I can picture the headline in the Camp Neeswaugee Newspaper," I said. *"Camper Beaten Senseless by Enraged Cabin Mate."*

"Come on, Curtis. You have to admit that was hilarious. *Yes! 'This shield is coming out perfect!'"* Kirk did a great impression of me, right down to looking around to see if anyone noticed.

"Shut up."

"It's a good thing you're gay, dude, because all those girls think you're a geek now."

"No one could ever think I'm a geek."

"I do."

"I'm going to pound you, Kirk."

"Ha! You just want to jump on me because I'm so sexy."

"As if!"

"Come on. You're a homo, so you know I'm sexy. All the girls want some of this," Kirk said, looking down at his own body.

Kirk was kind of hot, but I wasn't going to tell him that – for many reasons.

"Delusional much?"

"Yes!" Kirk mimicked me again.

"You're going to just keep doing that, aren't you?"

"Yes! Well, not forever, but it's good for a couple days at least."

"I hate you."

That just made Kirk laugh more.

My eyes narrowed when I spotted Elijah walking with Cody. I frowned. Elijah was trouble. He was short and had the face of an eleven-year-old, but he also had muscles. They were walking our way and would pass us in a matter of seconds.

Kirk noticed them, too. He looked sideways at me and smiled as I rolled up the sleeves of my shirt and puffed out my chest. When Cody and Elijah got close, I tensed my biceps and chest.

"Dude, you are so cool!" Kirk said to me so Cody could hear.

Cody looked in our direction.

"Hey," I said. "Sup?"

"We're off to Scouting," the boy of my dreams answered.

"Cool. I'm doing wrestling next."

"Oh! I want to try that!" Cody said.

Score!

Elijah frowned.

"Later!" Cody said as they continued on.

"Later!"

"Did you hurt yourself flexing?" Kirk asked when Cody and Elijah were out of earshot. "Wow, even I'm not that desperate to impress girls."

"You're more desperate."

"Ha!"

"I wish I was built like that Elijah kid," I said.

"Dude, you are way hotter than he is."

I turned and stared at Kirk.

"What? You think I can't tell if a guy is hot just because I'm into girls? I know when guys are hot. I just don't want to date them."

"Are you sure?" I asked, mischievously.

"Quit dreaming, Curtis. You aren't getting any of this," Kirk said and flexed. "Focus your efforts on someone you have a chance with, like pretty-boy Cody."

"So, now you think he's pretty."

"Listen, homo. Don't make me hurt you."

"Now, who's dreaming?"

Kirk just laughed. He laughed a lot. I liked that about him.

Kirk headed down to the soccer fields. My wrestling class was under a covered mat near main headquarters, so I went in and got a drink and then sat on one of the benches outside.

I despised Elijah. Not only did he have muscles, he possessed the advantage of sharing a class with Cody. I had to get close to that blond hottie so I could make a move. I was determined that when the dance rolled around I'd be dancing with Cody Studebaker.

I'd never wrestled before, but for me camp was about trying new things. There was no way I'd join a wrestling team, but a class at camp was different. If I didn't like it, I'd be done with it in two weeks, anyway.

I was in a class for beginners, which was fine by me. I was glad Elijah wasn't in my class. With his muscles he would probably have kicked my butt. Then again, if he was here he wouldn't be in Scouting with Cody, so getting my butt kicked would have been worth it.

If only Cody was in my wrestling class! I took a few moments to picture him in a singlet. Yum. Of course, we didn't wear singlets, but that didn't stop me from fantasizing about the blond hottie.

The counselor who taught wrestling was none other than my own Mr. Brubaker. I was right. He had been a wrestler in high school, and he was on the wrestling team at his university. He used me to demonstrate some moves. He took it easy on me, which was a good thing. Not only did I not know what I was doing, but Mr. Brubaker was about ten times stronger than I was. At one point my head was pressed into his chest, and I could feel his hard pecs flexing. I began to get excited, if you know what I mean. I rolled into a sitting position with my legs crossed so no one would notice.

Mr. Brubaker was hot. He was way older than I was, nineteen, but he had nice body. I'd been trying to get a look at him shirtless, but so far I'd only seen him in his staff shirt. His biceps strained the sleeves to the ripping point, and his chest pushed out his shirt so that the bottom of it hung down over his stomach like a curtain. I wished I looked like that! I had to force myself to quit thinking about his body and pay attention to what he was saying.

I was paired up with a boy about my size. I could read the fear in his eyes. I remembered what Kirk had said about some of the boys in the cabin being afraid of me because of my studded collar, but I wasn't wearing it right now. Mr. Brubaker had told us to take off all our jewelry at the beginning of class. I guess my natural bad-boy demeanor showed through.

I didn't smile at my opponent when Mr. Brubaker put us in our positions and blew his whistle. I figured a little intimidation would work in my favor.

The kid was strong, but no stronger than I was. I got him in a headlock within a few seconds and forced him onto his back a few seconds after that. I used my bodyweight to hold him down. I won!

It was just a class and not a real match, but Mr. Brubaker actually asked me if I'd wrestled at school. He seemed impressed when I told him I hadn't. He had me wrestle another opponent and told all the others in the class to watch how I was using the holds he had just taught us. I won my second match, too!

After class, Mr. Brubaker told me I should consider going out for the wrestling team at school. There was no way I was going to turn jock, but my chest swelled with pride when he told me I had natural talent. I was surprised I had any talent for wrestling. I wasn't into athletic stuff, except for skating, and I did that for fun, so I figured it didn't count.

My pride was still soaring later in the day when I returned to main headquarters for my last class: fencing. The class was held under the trees right by headquarters and not far from the wrestling ring.

I didn't think my mood could improve, but my eyes lit up with glee when Cody walked toward the fencing area. My heart pounded, and I hesitated to let myself hope, but he came straight toward me. Yes! Cody Studebaker was in my fencing class! Take that, Elijah!

"Hey," I said.

"Hey."

Cody grinned, and I went weak in the knees. I had a sudden urge to grab him and kiss him, but there was no way I could do that! Still, I could dream.

"How was wrestling?" Cody asked.

"Oh, wow! It was the best!"

I proceeded to tell Cody about my two wins and what Mr. Brubaker had told me about joining my school team.

"I didn't even think I'd be any good. I'd never wrestled before. Mr. Brubaker thought I had!"

"You must be a natural. I'm on the wrestling team back at school. Maybe I can give you some pointers."

"I'd love that! I'm really into wrestling now."

I wasn't as into wrestling as I pretended, despite my natural talent for it, but if it would get me close to Cody... wow. If we wrestled, I'd get to touch him. I had to keep myself from going further. I was getting too excited as it was.

Cody sat right down beside me and talked with me until class started. Some of the kids were staring at him. No doubt word had spread that Cody was a homo. A couple of the boys looked at him with nasty expressions on their faces, and a couple more were obviously uncomfortable near him. The others didn't seem to care. I wondered if it was because they really didn't care or just hadn't found out yet. Cody's popularity with the boys was sliding. Uncle Logan had told me that things used to be rougher for gay boys, but things still seemed pretty rough to me. I wasn't afraid. I could take care of myself, and if anyone tried picking on Cody I would kick his butt.

The girls paid more attention to Cody than ever, and that was saying something. He grinned whenever he noticed them watching him, but he kept his attention focused on me. I wasn't sure, but I thought he was flirting with me. He grinned at me a lot, flicked his hair out of his eyes in what I thought of as a flirty manner, and once licked his lips while he stared straight into my eyes. I was totally inexperienced in flirting, so I wasn't sure if he was really flirting or if I thought he was because I wanted him to flirt with me. Either way, I was sitting and talking to Cody Studebaker! Elijah no longer had an advantage over me, either. He shared a Scouting class with Cody, but I had fencing with him. Yes!

Fencing was way cool. It would have been more fun with swords, but I loved fighting with rapiers. It was a little hard to get used to the stances and staying inside the marked-off area, but fencing was my kind of sport. I felt like Captain Jack Sparrow from the *Pirates of the Caribbean* movies.

Cody and I got in a little bit of trouble while we were fencing together. I think he got caught up in a *Pirates of the Caribbean* moment, too, because we both kind of forgot what we were supposed to be doing and got into an all-out sword fight until Mr. Paré made us stop. Mr. Paré wasn't too mad at us, but he made us sit on the bench. Cody and I grinned at each other and almost started laughing. I never minded getting into trouble. It was quite often worth it. This was definitely one of those times.

Cody and I walked to the boys' area together after class. We started laughing about getting into trouble. It sent us into a giggling fit. Elijah spotted us as we were walking up into the cabin area, and best of all, Cody put his hand on my shoulder just then. Elijah was not a happy camper.

Cody and I went our separate ways, and I walked to Cabin 34. Kirk was already there. He mimicked me pumping my fist and saying, "*Yes!*" I threatened to pound him, but it did absolutely no good.

Jaden, one of my cabin mates, eyed me as he walked in and then went over to the other side of the center bins and began talking to two of the other boys while I told Kirk how Cody and I had gotten into trouble during fencing.

Jaden, Andy, and Todd whispered conspiratorially and kept looking over at me. I didn't pay much attention at first, but they kept it up.

"What?" I asked, brusquely. "If you have something to say to me, say it."

The three turned their heads in my direction. Andy had a somewhat guilty expression on his face. Todd scowled slightly. Jaden was defiant.

"I saw you with that Cody kid, the gay one. You two seemed *very* friendly."

"What's that supposed to mean?" I asked.

"You know what it means."

"Yeah, but I want to hear you say it to my face, unless that scares you."

Jaden came around the center bin, stopping when he was only about three feet away. Out of the corner of my eye, I saw Kirk move closer to me.

"It means I think you're a homo, too."

Andy looked kind of scared. Todd just watched with interest.

"You're absolutely right," I said.

"Faggot."

I was on Jaden so fast he didn't know what hit him, at least not until he figured it was my fist in his eye. Jaden punched me in the stomach, and we went down on the floor. I got in two more punches to his face, before Kirk grabbed me from behind and pulled me off. Todd grabbed Jaden, who was trying to get at me.

"Bring it on!" I said. "I'll kick your butt some more, loser!"

Mr. Brubaker came running up the steps, just in time to hear me call Jaden a loser.

"*You* and *you*, come with me *now*," he said, pointing to Jaden and me.

Mr. Brubaker led us down the hill to the shade of a large tree. I noticed Kirk, Todd, and Andy out on the front porch of Cabin 34, watching, but they were too far away to hear anything.

"He started it!" Jaden yelled before Mr. Brubaker could even say anything.

"He called me a faggot!"

"You are a faggot! You said so yourself!"

"Shut the he..."

"Stop! Both of you! Shut up and listen! It doesn't matter who started it or why. You are both in trouble. I will not tolerate fighting. Period."

"He slugged me in the..."

"Quiet!"

Mr. Brubaker turned to me.

"You! If you're involved in another fight, you're out of here!"

"But, I..."

"Shut it!"

Mr. Brubaker turned to Jaden.

"The same goes for you! And, if you call Curtis or anyone else that name or any other derogatory name, you are out of here!"

"But he is one!"

"You will not use that kind of language here. The same goes for you, Curtis. I heard what you called Jaden when I walked in."

"But he is one!" I said, mimicking Jaden. "Besides, what I called him isn't a tenth as bad as what he called me."

Jaden tried to get to me, but Mr. Brubaker stopped him with ease.

"Stop it! Both of you!"

"I'm not sleeping in the cabin with that...gay boy. He'll do stuff to me while I'm sleeping."

"Quit dreaming," I said.

"Shut up! I mean it! If he touches me, my parents will sue!"

"No one will touch anyone, Jaden."

"You couldn't pay me enough to touch him," I said.

"Shut up!" Jaden screamed at me.

I laughed out loud, and Mr. Brubaker scowled at me. I snapped my mouth shut.

"Neither of you are going to the movie tonight. You can sit in main headquarters with the counselor in charge until everyone comes back."

"That's not fair! He attacked me!" Jaden said.

"Yes, he did. You also verbally and then physically attacked him. That's why both of you are being punished."

Jaden growled. I started to grin, but Mr. Brubaker looked daggers at me, and I wiped the grin off my face really fast.

"Jaden, go see the nurse. Your face is beginning to swell. She'll give you an ice pack."

Jaden wanted to say something nasty, but instead he growled and walked toward the nurses' station.

"Do you need to go see the nurse, Curtis?" my counselor asked me.

"No. I'm not hurt *at all*," I said, making sure Jaden could hear it.

Jaden tensed, and his hands closed into fists, but he didn't look back and kept on walking.

"You need to learn to control your temper, Curtis," Mr. Brubaker said.

"I'm not putting up with anyone calling me *that* name," I said.

"You shouldn't have to, but punching him in the face isn't the way to handle it."

Half a dozen smart-alecky responses crossed my mind, but I wisely didn't say them out loud.

"So I'm just supposed to take it when some idiot calls me a faggot? Guys like me get pushed around all the time, and yeah, if you're wondering, I am gay."

"If someone here gives you trouble, you come to me or one of the other counselors. You don't take matters into your own hands. If you had controlled your temper and come to me instead, Jaden would be sitting out the movie and you'd be going with the rest of the boys. Instead, you did something just as unacceptable as he did."

I crossed my arms and scowled. I wanted to argue, but knew I wasn't on firm ground.

"Curtis, you can't let guys like Jaden get to you. You don't have to just take it, but you need to control yourself and take the appropriate action. Do you understand me?"

"Yes. He just made me so mad when he called me that. He was such an...he was being a real jerk about it."

"I'll keep an eye on him. If he gives you more trouble, come to me, but don't slug him again. Deal?"

"Deal."

I returned to the cabin while Mr. Brubaker joined the other counselors.

"So?" Kirk asked when I came back in.

"Mr. Brubaker sent Jaden to the nurse, and both of us have to sit in main headquarters tonight while everyone else is watching the movie."

"That is too bad, man, but it's probably worth missing the movie to pound Jaden's face."

"Yeah, but if I do it again, Mr. Brubaker said I'm out of here. He said he'd kick Jaden out if he calls me that again."

"Man, you let him have it," Kirk said. "You were on him before I even knew you were moving. Are all gay boys that tough?"

"I don't know many, but I'd have to say no."

Todd, Andy, and the other boys who were now in the cabin were listening while pretending they weren't. My entire cabin knew they were rooming with a homo now. None of them seemed to have much of a problem with it, unlike Jaden.

Jaden returned a few minutes later with an ice pack pressed to his face. His cheek was already swollen, and a black eye was beginning to form. I wanted to laugh at him, but I thought I'd better not. Jaden would probably go cry to Mr. Brubaker, and I'd be in even bigger trouble.

Despite staring a night of boredom in the face, I was in a good mood. I wished I'd had a little more time to beat the crap out of Jaden, but I was pleased with the punches I'd gotten in. Jaden hadn't left one mark on me. Pretty soon everyone would know we'd been in a fight, and they could tell just by looking that I'd kicked his butt.

My good mood evaporated when I spotted Elijah sitting beside Cody in the dining hall. Kirk and I were just coming out of the line with corn dogs, mashed potatoes, applesauce, and green beans when I spotted them together. Kirk noticed me scowling and headed right for their table. He took a seat to the right of Elijah, leaving a spot right next to Cody for me. I sat down, and Elijah frowned.

"I heard you got in a fight, but you don't look like you've been in one," Cody said.

"That's because I kicked the other guy's butt," I said. "A boy in my cabin called me a faggot, so I beat the crap out of him."

Cody gazed at me, and I could see the unspoken question on his lips.

"I don't mind being called gay. I am, after all. I don't even mind being called homo if it isn't being said in a nasty way. I don't like being called a faggot. Anyone who calls me that is going to pay."

I figured I might was well let Cody know I was gay. I wanted him, and it could only help my cause if he knew I was gay, too.

"I don't put up with it, either," Elijah said. "When the kids at school found out I was gay, I got pushed around and bullied until I punched a couple of guys in the face."

Elijah just *had* to announce he was gay. He couldn't stand the idea that I'd get any kind of advantage in our competition for Cody.

Kirk sneered at Elijah. I knew Kirk didn't like him simply because I didn't. Elijah went on to tell a story about being cornered by two football players and how he beat them both up. I figured it was a bunch of bull, but I didn't think I could call him on his crap without looking like a jerk.

"Jaden, the boy in my cabin who called me *that name*, had to go to the nurse, but I don't have a mark on me," I said.

"They had to call an ambulance for the football players I beat up. They couldn't play for the next two games," Elijah said.

Cody could tell I was annoyed. He seemed amused by our competing stories.

"There's Jaden now," I said pointing across the dining hall.

As Jaden drew closer his prominent black eye became noticeable. He also had a big bruise on his cheek.

"You did do a job on him," Cody said with admiration.

"I wish I could finish the job, but if I do I'll get kicked out of camp. Hmm, it might be worth it," I said and laughed.

Cody and Kirk laughed, too. Elijah glared at me.

I steered the conversation onto fencing, but near the end Elijah began talking about Scouting and conned Cody into helping him with some stupid junk for a merit badge. Elijah scratched the side of his head, giving me the finger, as they left together.

"I'm gonna get that guy," I said as they walked away.

Forty-five minutes later I stood with the off-duty counselors as everyone else departed to watch *Narnia: Prince Caspian*. I was bummed out because I really wanted to see that movie. I'd watched it at the theater, and it was totally cool. I loved anything with sword fighting, which is why I'd signed up for fencing.

"You'd better be on your way to main headquarters," said Mr. McNess, one of the counselors in our group. "Jaden is already there."

I nodded and walked in the general direction of main headquarters. Camp was eerily quiet. Almost everyone was heading to Eppley Auditorium to watch the movie. The off-duty counselors were taking the opportunity to escape from camp. Unlike us campers, they could go into town to do whatever it is counselors do.

I glanced around to make sure no one was looking and slipped into Cabin 31. Kirk had performed a spying mission for me just after supper and followed Elijah to see which cabin he was in. Later, I bribed Andy with a Hershey bar to go inside and find out which bed was Elijah's.

I moved swiftly and silently to Elijah's bed. I pulled off his blanket and top sheet, folded and hid the sheet between the mattress and the bed frame, then short-sheeted the bed. I'd never short-sheeted a bed before, but my uncle Logan had described how he'd done it when he was a counselor. I put the blanket back in place, and the bed looked just as it had when I started, only now there was only one sheet folded up to look like two. When Elijah tried to crawl into his bed he'd find it impossible. It wasn't a proper payback, but it was all I could think of on short notice.

I hurried down the hill and into main headquarters. The counselor on duty raised an eyebrow at my tardiness but didn't say anything. He just pointed to a chair at the side of the room. I sat down. Jaden was sitting in a chair facing me about ten feet away. He sneered at me. I had to disguise a laugh as a cough when I noticed his black eye and bruised face.

I had brought along a book to read and a notebook. I pulled a pen out of my pocket and opened the notebook. I wrote, "Nasty things to do to Elijah," across the top of the first page and began making a list. I giggled once as I was writing down ideas. The counselor scowled at me. Jaden shot me a look that clearly indicated he thought I was an idiot. I moved back to the top of the page and added, "and Jaden," to the title. I stared across the room and gave my cabin mate an evil grin.

When I ran out of ideas, I read for a while and then stared out the big front window of headquarters. I felt as if I'd been sitting there for hours, but only forty-five minutes had passed. My butt was numb, so I shifted in my chair. This had to qualify as cruel and unusual punishment.

I began reading again. My uncle had put a copy of *The Lightning Thief* in my bag. The story was pretty good, but I wasn't sure I'd tell my uncle that.

After an unbearable eternity, the counselor in charge looked up and told us we could go. My butt had no feeling in it at all when I stood up, and it was kind of hard to walk.

Jaden and I walked across the grass and up the hill together, just not too close. He didn't like me because I was gay, and I didn't like him because he was a prejudiced jerk. I wasn't one bit sorry I'd punched him in the face. I just wished I'd had a few more seconds to give him what he deserved.

"Prince Curtis has returned," Kirk said as I entered the cabin.

"Hey! Shut up! Don't remind me that I missed *Prince Caspian*," I said.

Kirk laughed.

"Have a good time?" he asked.

"It was a blast. Jaden and I spent the whole time making out."

"Mr. Brubaker!" Jaden yelled.

"Can't you even take a joke?" I said. "I wouldn't kiss you if you were the last boy on Earth."

Mr. Brubaker walked into the room. He gave me "the look," which meant he'd heard what I'd said from his quarters, and I was not quite in trouble but close enough that I'd better watch my step. I thought I detected the hint of a grin, too. I think he secretly liked what I'd said to Jaden.

Mr. Brubaker told us to go brush our teeth and to be back in ten minutes or less. So far, I liked Mr. Brubaker. He was generally pretty cool, even though he had made me miss the movie. I could see where he had to punish me. As much as Jaden deserved it, I could understand why Mr. Brubaker couldn't let me get away with pounding Jaden's face. He had given Jaden the same punishment, so that made it all okay.

"Okay, guys, get in bed, and I'll read. Once I start, no one talks," our counselor called from his room once we were all back.

I crawled into the top bunk and slid down in my sheets. With perfect timing, I heard a loud, "What the...?!!!", coming from the general direction of Cabin 31. I uttered an evil laugh, and Kirk grinned at me from across the room.

That's only the beginning, Elijah, I thought to myself.

Mr. Brubaker came out of his room carrying a book and a flashlight. It was the moment I'd been waiting for. I don't mean the book. Mr. Brubaker wasn't wearing a shirt! I checked him out before he turned off the lights. He had a wide, thick, well-muscled chest that narrowed down to a hard, flat abdomen. If that's the kind of body that wrestling created, maybe I'd have to really think about joining the team at school. I wanted to feel Mr. Brubaker's muscles so bad I couldn't stand it. Mr. Brubaker flipped off the light. I sighed.

"Once I start reading, there is no talking," Mr. Brubaker said.

"What happens if we talk?" I asked.

"You don't want to know."

"Oh, but I do!"

"No, you don't, Curtis. The last boy who talked while I was reading....well, you don't want to know that, either."

"Tell me!"

Mr. Brubaker turned on his flashlight, held it against his chest and shined it up on his face. It made him look creepy. I sat up on my elbows as he approached me. The other boys watched.

"If I tell you, you might never sleep again," Mr. Brubaker said.

"I want to know! I want to know!" I said and giggled.

"All I can say is, don't dig under the cabin," Mr. Brubaker said.

"Why not?"

"Just don't!"

"Come on, what happened to him?"

"The official story is he went home."

Mr. Brubaker laughed evilly.

"What *really* happened?" I asked.

"Like I said, don't dig under the cabin. That's all I'm saying."

I started to open my mouth.

"Zip it," Mr. Brubaker said quickly.

"But..."

"Zip it!"

I began to open my mouth again.

"Shh!"

"But..."

Mr. Brubaker stabbed his finger at me. We began a short game. I tried to get a word in before he could "shhh" me, but I couldn't do it. The other boys were giggling.

"Zip your lips, Curtis, or you'll find out exactly what happened to that boy."

I swallowed hard. Great, I had a psycho counselor. At least, he was hot.

"I'm going to read you a fantasy novel called *Foundation* by Mercedes Lackey. It's about a thirteen-year-old boy called Magpie."

Mr. Brubaker began to read, and no one talked. I really liked the story, but before I knew it, I fell asleep.

Chapter Three—I Stick My Foot in Something Nasty and Give a Fish to My Nemesis

Wednesday, August 11, 2010

Elijah eyed me suspiciously at breakfast the next morning. He suspected I was the one who short-sheeted his bed, but he couldn't know for sure. I had been in and out of his cabin in under three minutes, and I was reasonably sure no one had spotted me. I wasn't worried. It's not as if I'd get in much trouble for short-sheeting a bed. It was nothing compared to punching Jaden in the face, but it was nearly as much fun. I knew I really shouldn't have punched Jaden. The more I thought about it, the more I realized it wasn't right to hurt someone else. The next time, I'd control myself so that only Jaden would get in trouble.

My classes were a blast. Word had spread out from my cabin that I was gay. A few guys gave me the cold shoulder, some were jerks, and some were scared of me, but most didn't seem to care. The girls, on the other hand, liked it. They hadn't paid all the much attention to me before, but now I was popular. Kirk was in Heaven. He sat straight across from me, and females surrounded us.

"I saw you walking with Cody Studebaker. Are you two...an item?" one of the girls asked.

Every female eye in the tent turned on me, waiting for my answer. Some of the boys looked a bit jealous about all the attention I was receiving.

"Well...not exactly, but...we're heading in that direction."

"You guys would make such a cute couple! Two blond hotties together! Gay boys are soooo hot."

I laughed.

"Um...why would hetero girls think gay boys are hot?" I asked. I had always been genuinely perplexed about that one.

"They are usually sexy," one girl said.

"Or built," added another.

"Or both," said a third

"They take way better care of themselves than hetero boys, and they know how to dress," one of the girls said, casting a disparaging eye at the other boys in class. The boys noticed and didn't like it. Great, I was going to get beat up after class because they were jealous.

"One gay boy is hot, but two of them together? Come on, what's not hot about two boys kissing?"

"So, if I kissed Cody..." I said.

"I'd pay to watch!" one girl said and then held her hand over her mouth.

One of the counselors came close enough to hear, so we changed the topic. Counselors freaked out if the topic got anywhere near sex.

"Are you..." one of the girls asked Kirk.

Kirk looked confused for a moment, but then a look of comprehension crossed his face.

"No, uh...I like girls, but I'm cool with gay guys. Curtis is my best friend at camp."

"I'm impressed," another girl said. "Back at my school, the hetero boys are scared to death someone will think they're gay. They would never be friends with a gay boy. You must be really confident and secure."

Kirk grinned and blushed. It made him look especially cute.

"Cody Studebaker is the hottest boy in camp, and you're almost as hot, Curtis," one of the girls said.

"I am?"

I'd never thought of myself as especially hot. I thought I was good-looking, but more of an ordinary good-looking than hot.

"Yes, and you don't know you're hot, so that makes you even hotter."

"Well thanks for telling me I'm hot and ruining it for me then!" I said. "Now that I know, I'll lose that extra hotness that comes from not knowing I'm hot."

The girls giggled.

"You are hot, Curtis," Kirk said.

I highly expected he said it for the benefit of the girls. If so, it worked. A very pretty blonde girl scooted closer to Kirk.

"You're so fearless," she said. "I don't know any other boy who would have the courage to say that."

"Well, like I told Curtis before, hetero guys know when another guy is hot. Most just don't dare to say it out loud."

"You do. That's so attractive," the blonde said.

"The way I see it, why pretend I don't notice? I can think a guy is hot without being hot for him. Cody, for instance. He's hot, but I don't want him. I'd kill to have abs like his. Mine aren't bad, but he looks like he's done a zillion ab crunches."

"You've seen him without a shirt?" one of the girls asked.

The girls were all ears, and so was I.

"Yeah, he's ripped."

"You look kind of ripped yourself, Kirk," said the blonde.

"Oh, yeah!"

Kirk flexed his biceps, pretending to be a showoff. He was showing off, but he managed to pull it off as a joke, so it didn't look as if he was trying to show off.

I didn't know the names of any of the girls talking to us, but I was willing to bet Kirk would know quite soon.

We sat there all through Indian crafts, working on our projects and talking about cute boys. The other boys in class were totally jealous of Kirk. Maybe they'd learn that having a gay friend could pay off big.

When class let out, some of the girls walked with me a short distance and then veered off to their own classes. A couple of boys from class who had never spoken to me before said, "Hey," as they passed. Yeah, they were learning.

I had to wait on Kirk for a minute. He lingered in the Indian-crafts tent. Hetero boys were so slow!

"I think you should have to pay to hang out with me," I said. "I am a girl magnet," I said when he finally came outside, grinning.

"You're fooling yourself, Curtis. I'm the girl magnet. They love me because I'm confident and courageous enough to hang out with such a flaming homo."

"I'm going to punch you soon," I said.

Kirk laughed.

"I'm meeting up with Kayla at the dance!" Kirk said. He was so excited I feared he might pee his pants.

"Which one is she? All girls look alike to me."

"The blonde! She's so hot! I know you're gay, but you aren't blind!"

"Hey, I just didn't know her name."

"Two other girls have already said they want to dance with me, too."

"So that's why I had to wait for you outside the tent. You were arranging dates."

"I'm going to be surrounded by girls. I am the man!"

"It's all thanks to me. They like you because you're 'fearless' about being friends with a gay boy, but they would never know if you didn't have a gay boy to be friends with."

"Eh, this place is probably crawling with gay boys. I could replace you in an instant."

"Ha! As if!"

Kirk laughed yet again.

"Okay, I'll admit. The girls are a very nice fringe benefit to being your friend. I think I'll look for a gay friend at school. I'll have girls all over me!"

"Yeah, you'll just hate that, I'm sure."

Throughout the day, more and more girls talked to me. I received quite a bit of attention from girls back in school, but even more so here. Once I took note of the female attention, I also noticed that more girls than ever swarmed over Cody. His looks drew them in before the girls knew he was gay, but now...wow.

I couldn't get near Cody at lunch, but then neither could Elijah. He shot me a mischievous look that made me slightly nervous. He looked like someone who was up to something. I recognized the look with ease, because I was usually up to something myself.

I loved my wrestling class. I'd never been good at a sport before, but then I'd never tried before. Wrestling with other boys was kind of sexy, but I really was too focused on the match to think much about that. Some of the boys were a little reluctant to wrestle with a gay boy, but they relaxed when they figured out I wasn't trying to grab their butt.

I wished Jaden was in my class. I would have loved to get him on the mat. I'd totally humiliate him and not get in trouble for it.

Fencing was my favorite class, mostly because it was the one class I shared with Cody. We drew together whenever Mr. Paré told us to select an opponent. I hoped that meant Cody was interested in me.

Cody was a good fencer, even though he was a beginner like me. I paid way more attention in class than I normally would have because I wanted to impress Cody with my fencing prowess. We were pretty evenly matched, and I could hold my own with him.

"Wanna grab something at the canteen?" I asked Cody after class.

"Yeah, sure. I need a soda!"

I laughed.

The canteen was right by the wrestling mats. We each bought a Coke, and I led Cody out under the trees and sat down where we could speak alone.

"The girls in Indian crafts were talking about you. Well, they were talking about us," I said.

"About us?"

"They asked if we were an item. I told them no"

"So...you are gay."

I laughed.

"I said so the other day. Remember?"

Oh yeah! Sorry, I'm blond."

"Hey, so am I."

37

"Hey, you are blond. I hadn't noticed," Cody said, playing dumb. "I kind of thought you were gay even before you talked about fighting with that kid because of what he called you. You aren't obvious or anything, but sometimes when you look at me..."

"Well, you are very good-looking, Cody."

"Thanks."

Cody smiled but seemed a little uncomfortable. I was thinking about making a move but figured now was not the time.

"I talked with the girls in my Indian-crafts class about cute boys the whole period. They told me they think gay boys are hot."

"Yeah?"

"I asked them why, and they said we're usually sexy, built, or both, we take care of ourselves, and we know how to dress."

"It's all true," Cody said and laughed.

"Kirk told them you were ripped, and they got so excited."

"Is he..."

"No, he's a hetero, but he said he'd seen you without a shirt. Those girls are crazy for you. If you were straight, you could have them all."

"Ha ha, too bad I'm not, huh?"

"Well, I'm glad you're not."

I put my hand on Cody's leg for a moment, but I felt him tense, so I didn't keep it there long. I cursed myself. I knew it wasn't the time to make a move, so why did I do it? I wasn't thinking, that's why, and I was afraid Elijah would beat me to him.

"The girls really like Kirk because he's friends with me. They called him courageous and fearless. I think he already has three girls lined up for the dance. I told him he owes me."

"Hmm, I never noticed there was an advantage to having a gay friend."

"Well, you wouldn't, since you are gay," I said.

"Oh, yeah, that's true. Sometimes I...forget."

"You forget you're gay?"

"Uh...I just mean I forget that everyone isn't."

"Oh! Listen...this dance on Friday night...would you want to go with me?"

Cody's eyes widened for a moment, and he looked frightened, but the expression was gone so quickly I wasn't sure it had been there at all.

"I...um...I kind of said I would go with someone else. Well...we aren't really going together...not like a date or anything, but I promised Elijah we could hang out at the dance."

"Oh," I said, trying to keep the disappointment out of my voice.

"I guess I could hang out with you, too. Since the girls think gay boys are hot, three of us together will drive 'em nuts!"

I laughed.

"Hey, I have to get going, but yeah...we'll do the dance together."

"Cool. I'll walk you up the hill. We might as well give the girls a thrill."

"Yeah!" Cody said.

We stood and walked past main headquarters, the dining hall, an on toward the cabins. A lot of girls noticed us, and so did a few guys. We went our separate ways, and I headed on to Cabin 34.

I hated Elijah! It just figured he'd beaten me to Cody. I should have asked Cody to the dance before, but I didn't want to come off as desperate. Elijah was going to be in for a surprise when he found out I was going to be hanging out with Cody, too. I could block any move Elijah made. Unfortunately, it was going to be difficult to make any moves myself. Elijah would surely try to block me, too. If only I could get rid of that kid!

I kicked off my shoes and lay back on my top bunk staring at the ceiling. Maybe I could get Kirk to run interference for me at the dance, but no...he'd been too busy hitting on girls. I couldn't ask him to give up his prime, girl-hunting time. That's what straight boys lived for, after all. I'd have to come up with another idea.

I dozed off as I lay there. I slept and dreamed of Cody until Kirk shook me and told me it was getting close to suppertime. I climbed down out of my bunk and slipped my foot into my sneaker.

"What the...?"

"You looked like you just stepped in something nasty," Kirk said.

I pulled my foot out of my sneaker and looked inside.

"There's pudding in my shoes!"

The boys in the cabin burst out laughing, even Kirk. It was pretty funny, I guess. I could just imagine the look on my face. I still wasn't one bit happy I'd stuck my food in pudding! Mr. Brubaker chose just that moment to walk through the cabin.

"Most people use a bowl, Curtis," he said.

I glared at my counselor for a moment. I pulled my sock off. It was covered with vanilla pudding.

Jaden was laughing his butt off. I wanted to smack him, but of course I couldn't. I would have suspected he was the culprit, but I knew who was to blame.

"Elijah," I said under my breath so that only Kirk could hear. "This means war."

"Hmm," Kirk said, looking into my sneakers. "I prefer chocolate myself."

"Funny."

I usually changed shoes at lunchtime and again before supper. It was a trick Logan had taught me to keep my feet from getting so tired. It worked, too. I had changed shoes at lunch, so that meant someone, Elijah that is, had slipped in sometime between lunch and when I returned from classes.

"Did anyone see someone from another cabin in here after lunch?" I asked.

Everyone shook their head, but Jaden had a smirk on his face. I bet he'd seen Elijah come in. I bet he'd watched and laughed as Elijah put pudding in my shoes—the jerk.

I took my shoes up to the latrine and washed out my sneakers in the sink. It wasn't easy and I had to put up with "witty" comments from more than one boy. I managed to get all the pudding out, but I had very wet sneakers. I set them on the porch railing of the cabin to dry.

"So, Elijah, huh?" Kirk asked when he came out onto the porch.

"I'm sure of it. Jaden might have done it, but he's not smart enough to think of something like that. It was Elijah. I'm almost certain he knows I'm the one who short-sheeted his bed."

"So what are you going to do to him?"

"Oh, I have a plan."

"Can I help?"

"I was hoping you'd say that. The camp activity for tonight is a huge game of Capture the Flag. We can slip off and take care of Elijah. I will need supplies. Which would you rather track down—about a hundred small cups or a dead fish?"

"I think I'll handle the cups, but what are they for—and the fish?"

"You shall see. My uncle was a camp counselor here for years. He taught me all his dirty tricks."

"You must have one cool uncle."

"Yeah, but I'll never tell him that. Just get me the cups, and this evening we shall launch a two-pronged attack upon the enemy."

Kirk laughed.

"Are all gay boys this fun?"

"No. I'm special."

That evening Kirk and I slipped away from the massive Capture the Flag game that was being played on the soccer fields between the boys' and the girls' area. Jaden had called it "Capture the Fag," but he said it when only I could hear.

Kirk went into our cabin where he'd stashed a whole bag of small paper cups. I retrieved the fish I'd found on the shore near the lake and carefully sealed in a plastic bag. Next, I borrowed a large bucket from the cleaning-supply closet in the latrine and filled it with water.

Kirk and I walked the short distance to Cabin 31 and darted inside. So far, so good.

I took the fish out of bag, taking care to touch it only with the plastic of the bag itself. Kirk watched with interest to see what I was going to do with it.

"Hold up the mattress, but don't disturb the sheets," I said.

A confused expression crossed Kirk's face, but he did as I said. I carefully slipped the dead fish under the mattress, placing the plastic bag on top both so I wouldn't have to get my hands fishy and to keep the mattress from being ruined.

"Okay, done."

Kirk lowered the mattress. The bed looked perfectly normal.

"In a day or two, that fish will really start stinking up the place," I said.

Kirk laughed.

"You're uncle taught you this?"

"Yeah. I think he was evil when he was a counselor. He's a good role model."

"Okay, what are we doing with the cups?"

"Start filling them with water and place them all around the bed."

The light went on above Kirk's head.

"Oh! I get it!"

We worked the next several minutes filling cups with water and putting them all around Elijah's bed.

"This is a lot of work!" Kirk said.

"Yes, but it will be just as much work for Elijah to get rid of them."

"Dude, this is fun. I'm glad you're feuding with him."

"Hey, he's after my boyfriend!"

"You wish Cody was your boyfriend."

"Well, he's after Cody, who I want to be my boyfriend. At the very least, I want to dance with him and make out with him, and Elijah is getting in my way."

"That fish is going to be so rank. I'm glad I'm not your enemy."

I grinned.

We finished the job, replaced the bucket, and raced down the hill to join the game.

"Whoa, he took off his shirt," I said.

"Who?

"Who do you think? Cody! He is so buff. Yum!"

"Dude, you're drooling," Kirk said.

I quickly wiped my mouth and then realized I'd been tricked. I gave Kirk a dirty look, but he just grinned at me.

We rejoined the game, on Cody's side. I spent most of my time staying near him just so I could check him out. His chest was perfect and his abs... Wow! He was so defined. Cody even looked sexy from the back. I never thought much about a guy's back, but his was wide and muscled.

Cody was the favorite target of the girls on the other team. They no doubt wanted to get close to get an eyeful, too. Elijah was right there, too, of course. I grinned at him to make him nervous and so he'd know for sure later that I was the one who put water cups all around his bed. I hoped he wouldn't discover the fish for at least a couple of days. With any luck, it would merely be a bad odor with an unknown source before it became so nasty it was easy to locate. Logan said that was the beauty of the fish treatment. It kind of slips up on the victim.

Capture the Flag was a blast! Cody, Kirk, and I joined up, much to Elijah's dismay, and mounted an attack. We darted in as a team and gave the opposing team three targets to track. We didn't get very close to the flag, but all I really cared about was sticking close to Cody so I could check out his sexy, sweaty body.

When Cody, Kirk, and I made another coordinated attack, Mr. Brubaker, who was playing for our team, used us as a distraction, grabbed the enemy flag, and raced back. The three of us switched tactics and blocked as many of the enemy as possible. Even the fastest kids couldn't match Mr. Brubaker, and soon he was waving the enemy flag from the safety of our base. He'd captured the flag, and we had won!

It might not seem fair that we had a counselor on our team, but there were counselors on both teams, so it all evened out. Mr. Brubaker was smart for a jock. He watched and awaited his chance. He didn't dart in for the enemy flag until the counselors on the opposing team were too far away to catch him.

Cody gave me a high five, and we all headed back for the cabins. Kirk and I grinned at each other. Soon, Elijah would find the way to his bunk blocked by a hundred cups of water. More fun to think about was the fish, slowly becoming more and more rank, hidden under his mattress. Cody probably wouldn't smell it at all tonight, but soon the stench would begin.

Chapter Four—My Boxer Briefs Rise to New Heights, and My Archenemy Gets a Surprise in His Underwear

Thursday, August 12, 2010

The dance was only one day away. I didn't usually get excited about dances. They aren't my thing, but it wasn't the dance itself that was important. It was being with Cody. If I was with him at the dance, it meant he was mine. There was one huge problem with that idea: Elijah. If it weren't for Elijah, I'd have Cody all to myself. He was my sole competition for Cody Studebaker. There had to be other gay boys at camp, but they were obviously afraid to make a move. I wished Elijah was more timid. He didn't look all that tough, but he was bold. I hated that!

I was going to the dance with Cody, but so was my archenemy. Maybe I'd get lucky and Elijah would fall in poison ivy or get into big trouble and be sent home. I momentarily thought of jumping him right before the dance and tying him to a tree, but that probably wasn't a wise idea. Sure, it sounded like fun, but I'd end up getting kicked out of camp, and then Elijah would have Cody all to himself. He'd just love that.

I walked down to the dining hall with Mr. Brubaker and my cabin mates for breakfast. We had French-toast sticks with syrup, scrambled eggs, bacon, and toast.

I spotted Elijah sitting with his cabin mates and wondered if he'd discovered the fish yet. I put my tray down and started back for some orange juice. I couldn't resist taunting Elijah just a bit.

"Hey, Elijah. I'm getting some juice. Can I get you anything? A cup of water, perhaps?"

Elijah gave me a dirty look. If he didn't know who'd pranked him before, he did now.

"I'm good," he said.

I eyed Elijah cautiously. He was just a little too happy. I'd say he was even pleased with himself. I walked on, feeling a little uneasy.

"Hey, Curtis!" Elijah called out. "I think your boxer-briefs are rising."

I felt the back of my shorts, fearing my underwear was showing, but everything was fine. I looked at Elijah. He and his cabin mates were laughing. How did Elijah even know I wore boxer-briefs?

I got my juice and went back to my table.

"That was lame," I said.

I started in on my French-toast sticks, but one of the boys from my fencing class called out to me as he walked past our table with his tray.

"Hey, Curtis! Nice underwear!"

Some of the boys with him laughed. Kirk and I looked at each other. He didn't get it, either. I wondered what was going on.

I began to get uncomfortable. Way too many people were looking at me and laughing. I couldn't stand it after a while and stood up.

"Kirk, is there anything wrong with my underwear? Am I wearing a sign on my butt or something?"

Kirk checked me out and shook his head. I sat back down.

"What is going on?" I asked. "I don't like this. Elijah is up to something. I just know it."

I finished my breakfast. Kirk and I got up with our trays. A lot of kids were looking in my direction and giggling. Even some of the counselors were grinning.

My heart began to beat faster. Cody Studebaker walked toward me. He looked so cute in his khaki shorts and Camp Neeswaugee T-shirt. I had to get a picture of him to take home with me!

"Uh, Curtis. I think you'd better go check the flagpole," Cody said quietly once he reached me.

I gave him a confused looked.

"Just do it," Cody said.

Kirk and I dumped our trays and headed toward the flagpoles located between the dining hall and main headquarters. I looked up. There was the American flag, the Indiana State flag, and...my neon-yellow boxer-briefs flying in the breeze. At the bottom of the flagpoles was a poster board sign that read, "Curtis, I hope you're enjoying camp. I thought you might need these in case you have another accident. ~Love, Mom."

Tears welled up in my eyes. I turned and walked quickly away. Kirk followed, looking both surprised and worried. I passed Mr. Brubaker as I hurried away from the flagpoles.

"Curtis? Are you okay?" he asked.

I just shook my head and kept walking as the tears began to stream down my cheeks. I didn't want anyone to see me cry. Kirk was gazing at me, concern etched on his face.

I kept on walking, all the way to the huge oak at the bottom of the boys' area. I couldn't stop the tears.

"Curtis...everyone will forget about it by lunch. Look, Mr. Brubaker is already taking them down. It was just a joke. No one is going to believe you wet your pants. They might tease you, but... I don't understand why you are so upset."

"It's not the underwear or the prank," I said. It was hard to talk because I was sobbing.

"Then..."

"My mom is dead! Okay? My parents were killed in an accident a few months ago."

I stood there crying, feeling weak and embarrassed.

"Oh, crap. I'm sorry, Curtis. I'm sure Elijah didn't know. I know you guys don't like each other, but he wouldn't have done that if he'd known."

I wiped my tears away.

"I know. I'm not mad at him. It just hit me when I read that sign. I'm okay most of the time, but sometimes..."

I started to tear up again. Kirk put his hand on my shoulder, then hugged me for a few moments.

"I hope no one saw me crying."

"I don't think anyone saw you except for Mr. Brubaker."

"I hope not. I don't want everyone thinking I'm a big wuss because I started crying over a practical joke. It was pretty funny. I'm kind of ticked off that Elijah beat me to it. I was planning on running *his* underwear up the flagpole."

Kirk laughed.

"I'm sure you'll think of something."

"Oh, I already have."

I grinned through my tears that were already stopping.

"Are you going to be okay?" Kirk asked.

"Yeah. That sign just hit me wrong. I think about my parents every day, but that sign brought all the pain back. My mom can't send me notes at camp because she's gone..."

"If anyone did see you crying, and I don't think anyone did except our counselor, I'll tell them why. No one is going to think you're weak if they know the truth. It would make me cry, too, man. I don't want to even think about...well, I've got your back, okay?"

"Thanks."

"Besides, no one will give you a hard time about crying anyway. They'll be too afraid you'll kick their butt."

I laughed.

We walked up the hill towards Cabin 34.

"Of course, I am going to make Elijah pay for running my underwear up the flagpole and for hinting that I wet my bed."

"What are you going to do to him?"

I laughed evilly and then whispered into Kirk's ear.

"Oh, man! Oh! Wow! I've said it before, but I'm glad I'm not your enemy."

I just smiled in response.

When we neared the cabin, Kirk spotted Mr. Brubaker and headed in his direction. I knew he was going to tell him why I'd lost it. I was glad I didn't have to explain. Kirk was a really good friend.

"Nice underwear, Curtis!" Jaden said as I walked in.

"At least mine aren't all crusty, Jaden."

"Ohhh!" said a couple of our cabin mates.

Jaden sneered at me.

I had to endure underwear comments all morning, but oddly no one even mentioned the bed-wetting hint, maybe because almost everyone had wet their bed at one time or another. I had to admit it was a good joke. Better, it gave me an excuse to retaliate.

I pretended I had to go to the bathroom right before the end of the 4th period, which was just before lunch. I raced back to the cabin, grabbed what I needed, then sneaked into Cabin 31. I did my dirty work quickly and then took a moment to check on the fish. It was still hidden under the bed, and it was beginning to smell. I slipped out of Elijah's cabin without being seen. I grinned as I walked leisurely to Cabin 34.

"Did you do it?" Kirk asked later as we walked down to lunch together.

"Yes. Now, all we have to do is wait."

I didn't care for the look of the roast beef au jus as Kirk and I passed through the line, so I took my tray and headed for the salad bar. I made myself a big salad with lots of cheese and got some applesauce and vanilla pudding. Kirk rejoined me, and we headed for Cody's table. Elijah was already sitting beside him. I sat down on Cody's other side. Elijah grinned at me, obviously pleased with himself.

"That was a good one," I said.

"I don't know what you're talking about," Elijah said, feigning innocence.

"Just be warned...expect it when you least expect it."

Elijah looked slightly fearful, but he tried not to let it show. I enjoyed messing with his mind. He'd be looking over his shoulder until the ax fell. I couldn't wait, but then again, I enjoyed the paranoid look in Elijah's eyes.

Cody started to get up, but Elijah stopped him.

"You need something? I was just going to go get some...pudding."

"Yeah, could you get me another brownie?" Cody asked.

"Sure."

Elijah got up and walked away.

"And some pudding, too!" Cody called after him.

Kirk and I exchanged a glance. Elijah was so pathetic.

"Hey, Curtis. Could you make me one of those cool wristbands in Indian crafts?" Cody asked. "I should have taken that class."

"Yeah, sure."

"Cool. Maybe something in red, black, white, and turquoise."

"No problem."

"That's really nice of you, Elijah...I mean Curtis," Kirk said.

I looked at him and mouthed, "Shut up." He merely grinned.

During lunch, Cody sent Elijah off for yet another brownie, a carton of juice, and a glass of lemonade. Cody didn't ask Elijah to be his waiter. Every time Cody started to stand, Elijah jumped up like a trained monkey.

Elijah and I made nice in front of Cody. Anyone walking by would have thought Cody, Kirk, Elijah, and I were best buddies. I was dying to make fun of Elijah for being Cody's personal serving boy, but I couldn't.

The number of girls who grinned at Cody as they passed was amazing. He smiled, winked, and flirted back. He obviously loved the attention. I noticed one very cute boy giving Cody the eye, too, and I didn't like it. I did not need more competition!

Kirk and I got up to dump our trays near the end of lunch period.

"Could you take mine, too?" Cody asked.

"Sure."

There was no way I was going to let Elijah get ahead of me.

Kirk waited until we were outside to make fun of me.

"'I'll be happy to make you a wristband'. 'Sure, I'll take your tray'. 'Will there be anything else, sir?'" Kirk asked. "You are so whipped, dude."

"I'm not whipped. Elijah is whipped. He's Cody's personal serving boy. Did you see how he jumped up every time Cody moved? He's so pathetic."

"And you aren't?"

"Shut up!"

"Maybe you'll get lucky and Cody will let you make his bed."

"Shut up."

Kirk laughed.

"Before the end of camp, you two will be his personal slaves and probably love every minute of it."

"I'm no one's slave, but I'm not letting that little jerk get ahead of me. If that's the game he wants to play, I'm in."

"I'd say Cody is the one playing the game."

"He's enjoying it, I'm sure, but Elijah started it."

"Is Cody even worth it, Curtis?"

"Have you seen him without a shirt? Have you looked into his eyes?"

"Whoa! Calm down there, tiger! I think you're about to drool."

"Besides, it doesn't matter if Cody is worth it or not. I have to win."

"So this is about you being freakishly competitive and not about your huge crush on a boy?"

"It's about both, jerk." I grinned. "I want Cody and I mean to have him. I'm not about to let Elijah get him instead."

"Does that mean that if you fail to get Cody you plan to off him so Elijah can't have him?"

"I might be a tiny bit obsessed. I'm not deranged."

"Of course, you're not," Kirk said in a soothing voice as if he was talking to a mental-hospital patient.

"Hey, this is summer camp. Nothing really matters here. In less than two weeks it will all be over, so what anyone thinks about me doesn't matter at all, not that I care much about what others think," I said.

"So you're saying you're willing to make a complete fool of yourself because you'll never see any of us again, at least not until next summer?"

"I'm saying that if I do make a fool of myself, or people hate me, or I get publicly humiliated by say...having my neon-yellow boxer-briefs ran up the flagpole...then I only have to deal with it until the end of camp. Of course, someone here might end up attending my school."

"I don't think that last bit is likely," Kirk said.

"Ha! My uncle and his boyfriend met here when they were counselors, and that's exactly what happened."

"It's kind of cool your uncle is gay. I guess that means he doesn't give you any trouble."

"Oh, he gives me lots of trouble, just not about being gay: *'Don't drink out of the milk carton, Curtis.' 'Leave your door open when you have a boy in your room, Curtis.' 'Do your homework, Curtis.' 'No, you can't stay out until 2 a.m., Curtis.'* It's a nightmare!"

"Hmm, sounds a little like my dad, except I can't have girls in my room at all."

"I bet he lets you have boys in your room with the door closed."

"Yeah, but that's only because he knows I'm not a big homo like you."

"Eh, it's okay. I'll hang out with you, anyway, even if you aren't cool enough to be gay."

"Wow! Thanks, Curtis! You're soooo selfless!"

"What can I say? My middle name is selfless."

"Yeah, sure it is."

"Curtis?"

"Yeah?"

"Have you kissed a boy?"

"Yeah. I had a boyfriend back home for a while. We made out. Why?"

"I'm just wondering if it's different from kissing a girl. I've kissed girls, but it seems like it would be different with a guy."

"I've never made out with a girl, so I don't know if it's different or not. Is there something you aren't telling me, Kirk?"

"No. I'm not secretly gay. I just kind of wonder how it's different."

"I can give you all the details about kissing a boy if you want," I said mischievously. "Maybe even a personal demonstration."

"No, thank you, unless you want to hear all the details about kissing a girl."

"Eww! Eww! No way! It's bad enough seeing a boy and girl kiss; what a disgusting heterosexual display."

Kirk laughed.

***

The next bit of excitement came after supper. Kirk and I were in the cabin debating with some of the other boys on what evening activity to choose when a scream and a string of words that should not be used in camp drowned out our discussion. I recognized Elijah's voice.

Kirk and I looked at each other and grinned. We turned and looked out the screen-windows in time to see Elijah running out of Cabin 31, wearing only tighty-whities and flip-flops. He made a dash for the latrine.

"I figured he wouldn't change his underwear until tomorrow morning," I said.

Kirk and I burst into laughter. We laughed until our eyes watered, rolling around on my top bunk like maniacs. Mr. Brubaker came out and looked at us as if we'd lost our minds.

We kept watch, and a few minutes later Elijah came back out of the latrine, now wearing only his flip-flops. He was carrying his briefs.

He glared at our cabin just before he went inside his own.

Kirk and I started giggling again. It was just too funny.

A very few minutes later, a fully dressed Elijah came stomping down the hill and up the steps of our cabin. The door flew open, and he stood there glaring at me with his fists clinched.

"I know you did it!" he said. "You will pay, Curtis Lincoln! You will pay!"

With that he turned and left.

"I see you're making new friends, Curtis," Mr. Brubaker said.

"I have no idea what he was talking about," I said, putting on my best innocent look.

"Uh-huh," said Mr. Brubaker and then walked into his room.

"What did you do?" Jaden asked.

Jaden rarely spoke to me, but his curiosity got the best of him.

"I put *Icy Hot* in his underwear in retaliation for running my boxer-briefs up the flagpole."

"Oww!" Jaden said.

Half the boys in the cabin put their hands over their crotches and had pained expressions on their faces. It was the same reaction most guys had when they saw another guy get hit in the 'nads.

"The best part is it won't wash off. It will burn for hours," I said.

"You are pure evil," Jaden said. Oddly enough, there was a touch of admiration in his voice.

Mr. Brubaker came out of his room and walked over to me.

"Hand it over," he said.

I played dumb and innocent. It didn't work.

"*Now*, Curtis."

I sighed, climbed down off my bunk and retrieved the jar of *Icy Hot* I had hidden in my center bin. I'd forgotten Mr. Brubaker could hear everything we said from his room. I was busted.

"Outside," he said.

Kirk gave me a look of pity as our counselor led me outside.

Mr. Brubaker stood and faced me. His muscles were intimidating.

"Don't do it again," he said.

I nodded.

"Putting *Icy Hot* in someone's underwear could be dangerous."

"I didn't mean to hurt him...much."

"Practical jokes aren't funny if someone gets hurt. I know you understand that."

He was referring to the note on the flagpole this morning. Elijah had no idea how much his joke had hurt me. I nodded again.

"Think before you act, Curtis. Don't take things too far. I like you, and I want you to be able to stay here."

"Okay, I'm sorry."

"Just remember what I said. Don't do it again."

I nodded. Mr. Brubaker walked away, and I released a sigh of relief. I thought for a moment that I was in big trouble.

I walked back into the cabin. All the boys were watching me.

"He wasn't happy," I said.

"Are you getting kicked out of camp?" Jaden asked.

"No."

Jaden didn't seem too disappointed. I don't think he hated me quite as much as he had.

"Maybe we should start a pool and guess the date on which you'll get booted out of camp," Kirk said.

"Who me? I never cause trouble."

Kirk rolled his eyes, then laughed.

Chapter Five—Elijah Gives Me a Makeover from Hell

Friday, August 13, 2010

If looks could kill, I would have dropped dead right there in the dining hall. Elijah glared at me as I sat down on the other side of Cody.

"Good morning, Elijah," I said cheerfully.

Whenever Cody was watching, Elijah made nice, but whenever he wasn't, it was quite apparent that Elijah wanted me dead. He even mouthed, "I hate you." I just grinned at him, mainly to tick him off.

"How's my wristband coming along?" Cody asked.

"I did the design, strung up the loom, and I've got about a fourth of it finished."

"Could you get it done by tonight – for the dance? You could give it to me there."

Cody smiled at me. He even reached out and touched my arm. I went all weak and wobbly.

"Sure," I said. Why I said it, I don't know. I'd have to work my butt off to get it done.

Kirk rolled his eyes when I looked at him.

Elijah took care of Cody as if he was his personal waiter. It was so pitiful. I momentarily pictured Elijah as a little dog on a leash, panting and pawing at Cody's knee. I laughed out loud, and Elijah looked at me as if I was a freak.

I took Cody's tray along with mine when I left. I could feel Kirk looking at me. After we dumped our trays and walked outside, I turned to him.

"Okay, let me have it. I know you're dying to make fun of me, so get it out of your system."

"'Oh, yes, Cody, I'll finish your wristband by tonight, anything for *you*'," Kirk said in a simpering voice.

"I do not sound like that, and all I said was 'sure'."

"Your mouth said 'sure', but your expression said all the rest. You are so sad."

"Hi, Kirk. Hi, Curtis," Kayla said as she headed toward the girls' area.

"Hi, Kayla. I'll see you in class," Kirk said in a dreamy voice.

"Now who is pathetic?" I asked when Kayla had passed us. "Your tone was so sickening sweet I'm about to overdose on sugar."

"Hey, I'm not making her a wristband like you are for your dream boy. Wait, do you think she'd like one?"

"You are so pathetic, you know that?" I asked.

"She's soo sexy and that blonde hair...wow."

"I have blond hair."

"Yeah, but you're a guy. You don't count."

"Fine, but you're still pathetic."

"So are you."

"Then we'll be pathetic together."

"Yeah!"

I laughed. Kirk was always fun.

***

I worked feverishly on Cody's wristband during Indian crafts. Kirk kept mouthing, 'Oh, Cody', and I glared back at him.

Kayla sat right next to Kirk during class. There is no way he could make her a wristband before the dance, but I noticed he was working on a bracelet using pink and white beads. Those were definitely not Kirk's colors, so I knew he was making it for Kayla.

We were surrounded by girls, which made the boys draw closer. The boys in class had never been rude to me, but now they went out of their way to be nice. They all wanted in on what Kirk had: popularity with the girls because he had a gay friend. Who would have thought that being a homo would make hetero boys buddy up to me?

I took my loom and a small supply of beads with me when class was over so I could work on Cody's wristband whenever I had free time. I had to get it finished by the dance!

Kirk actually put his arm around Kayla as we walked down the hill. Suddenly, I was a third wheel, but I didn't mind. I figured pathetic straight boys need all the help they could get.

At lunch, Elijah had a smirk on his face that made me nervous. He was up to something again, but then I knew he'd retaliate. I was uneasy wondering just what he'd do, but I tried not to let it show. The last thing I wanted to do was let him know he was getting to me. I occupied my mind by checking out Cody and thinking about how I'd be dancing with him in only a few hours. My thoughts of Cody made me smile, and my smile confused the heck out of Elijah.

I used all my spare time to work on Cody's wristband. One of the instructors had cut the leather for it during class and I'd borrowed a glover's needle and some nylon thread. I had everything I needed to complete it, except perhaps time. I carried the loom everywhere with me. It was my constant companion. I watched it closely whenever Elijah was around. I didn't want to give him any chance to sabotage it. One cut string would spell disaster.

Wrestling class didn't go quite as smoothly as usual. I took an elbow to the face during a match. It was an accident, but it hurt. Mainly, I was worried that it would leave a bruise. That's why I didn't argue when Mr. Brubaker sent me to the nurse for an ice pack. I wanted to look good for the dance.

I was kicking butt in wrestling. A couple of the boys had been hesitant to wrestle a homo, but they wised up and figured out I was all business. I'll admit, if I was wrestling Cody or someone of equal hotness, I might have used the opportunity to do a little exploring, but the boys in my class weren't all that hot. They had nothing to worry about from this gay boy.

I was good enough that guys my size were intimidated by the idea of wrestling me. Mr. Brubaker matched me against some bigger guys and used the opportunity to show the class ways in which a smaller guy could defeat a bigger one. I did pretty well against guys with quite a bit more muscle, but I lost most of my matches with them. I was surprised when I beat any of them, and so were they!

Fencing was still the best! Most of that was because I shared the class with Cody, but Mr. Paré said I had a lot of swashbuckler in me. He usually split up Cody and me because we tended to forget what we were supposed to be doing and got a little crazy when we were together. Mr. Paré wasn't all that amused when we started acting out fight scenes from *Pirates of the Caribbean*.

I wanted to kiss Cody so badly. When I looked at his lips, an irresistible force drew me toward them. It was as if I was meant to kiss him! I was pulled toward him by pure instinct. If things went well at the dance I might try to kiss him, but I was going to take things one step at a time. If we danced together, it would be the first time I'd ever danced with another boy, in public or private, and tonight would be very public indeed.

I walked with Cody towards the cabins after class. Elijah joined us at the flagpoles. Cody put an arm around each of our shoulders while a big group of girls was watching.

"You should take fencing, Elijah. We could be the three musketeers," Cody said.

Yeah, that would work. I'd run Elijah through with a rapier if he didn't get me first. That didn't quite strike me as the spirit of 'one for all and all for one'.

Cody seemed completely oblivious to the mutual hatred between Elijah and me. Hatred might be too strong a word for it. It's not as if we wanted each other dead. Sometimes I thought that I wanted him dead, but I didn't really. I even felt a little guilty for putting *Icy Hot* in Elijah's briefs. We didn't hate each other. We just disliked each other.

Hate or dislike, Cody couldn't see it. I don't know how he missed the nasty looks and general atmosphere of hostility, but he did. Of course, Elijah and I tried to hide our mutual dislike from Cody, because neither of us wanted to look bad in front of him.

So...the three of us walked up the hill, looking like best buddies, instead of like two rivals fighting over the hot boy in the middle. I wanted Elijah to disappear, but he was the price I had to pay for being near Cody, at least for now.

My wardrobe was severely limited at camp, but after I returned to my cabin, I spent a good half hour trying to pick out the right shirt and shorts for the dance that night. Kirk looked up from his magazine from time to time to watch me. Finally, he threw his magazine on his bunk, jumped up, and walked over to me.

"I can't stand it anymore! Just wear the royal blue one! You look good in it. I can't believe anyone can take so long to pick out a shirt!"

"I'm also picking out shorts."

"They're all the same!"

"Not to anyone who cares about clothes."

"Here, you're wearing these!" Kirk said, grabbing a pair and shoving them at me.

"I don't know..."

"Wear them or I'll put *Icy Hot* in your underwear!"

"Okay, okay. You're awfully dramatic for a straight boy."

"Oh, shut up."

"I'm going to take a shower," I said, stripping off my shirt.

I got naked and wrapped a towel around my waist. I grabbed my shower caddy and made sure it contained my wild-violet shampoo, special conditioner for my spiked hair, and my sweet-pea body wash. I took a washcloth out of my bin and walked up the hill to the showers.

There were only four boys taking a shower, but then this wasn't one of the times when we were forced to do so. I liked to take my shower in the morning, but I wanted to look extra good for the dance.

I'd been hoping to catch Cody in the shower, but so far it had never happened. His cabin wasn't close to mine, and there were three latrines with showers, so he probably used a different one. I had considered checking out the other showers, but since I was out at camp, the boys might think I was there to check them out. That would kind of be true, but I'd really be there to check out Cody. Most of the boys in camp were just boys and didn't have anything I wanted to see, clothed or naked. Cody was special.

I lathered up my hair, enjoying the wild-violet scent. I'd picked the shampoo because it was purple, which was my favorite color, but it smelled really good, too. I rinsed the shampoo out then grabbed my leave-in conditioner. When I squirted it out in to my hand it looked darker than I remembered. I sniffed it. It smelled okay. Could conditioner go bad? I mentally shrugged and worked it into my blond hair.

I washed off with my body wash. Jaden had teased me about my sweet-pea body wash until I held up the bottle and told him it could also act as a suppository. He didn't get it until he asked Mr. Brubaker later. My counselor just looked at me and shook his head in disbelief, or was it frustration?

The hot water was relaxing. I liked showering when there weren't so many boys in the showers. Fewer boys meant hotter water. When everyone was trying to shower all at once, the water was no more than lukewarm, and I liked it hot!

I rinsed off my body, taking care not to get my hair wet. I reluctantly turned off the shower, then walked over to the benches and grabbed my towel off its hook. I dried off and wrapped the towel around my waist.

When I returned to the cabin, everyone was out. I slipped on a pair of blue boxer-briefs, and since Kirk wasn't there to annoy me, draped three shirts over the side of my bed so I could see which would look best. I stood there in my briefs for about ten minutes before I decided that the one Kirk picked was the best, after all. It also possessed the added advantage of hiding the fact that I'd spent yet more time picking out clothes for the dance.

I pulled on the pair of cargo shorts Kirk had picked out and slipped on some sandals. I was about to check myself out in the mirror when Jaden walked in. He looked at me so oddly I just stared at him.

Kirk came pounding up the steps but stopped dead when he looked at me.

"What did you do to your hair?" he asked.

"I shampooed it. You should give it a try sometime, Kirk."

"Funny, but what did you do to it?"

"What do you mean what did I do to it? I told you. I shampooed it and put on my conditioner. Oh! I forgot to spike it! Where's my gel?"

"Why did you dye it?" Kirk asked.

I looked at him, totally confused.

"Dye it?"

"Yes, dye it. Your hair was blond, now it's black."

"Funny, Kirk."

He just kept looking at me. Jaden began to laugh. I rushed over to the mirror.

"What the... NOOOOO!"

I grabbed my conditioner, opened the top, and looked inside. It was a lot darker than it should have been. It wasn't going bad. Someone had messed with it.

"Elijah," I said out loud.

I began ripping off my clothes and tossing them on my bunk. I grabbed my shampoo and my towel and ran out of the cabin and up to the showers. I turned on the water and shoved my head under. I shampooed and rinsed, then shampooed and rinsed again. I walked over to a mirror and looked at my reflection. It was no good. My blond hair was now black.

I dried off and walked out of the showers. Elijah and some of his cabin mates were out on their porch.

"Nice hair, Curtis!" Elijah called out.

I glared at him but didn't say anything. They all laughed as I walked away. I clenched my fists and kept walking.

When I returned to the cabin, I walked over the mirror and gazed at my reflection. Kirk was watching me.

"It won't wash out," I said. "I'm going to have black hair for the rest of camp."

"It doesn't look bad, Curtis," Kirk said. "It's just not blond."

I was none too happy. I dressed once more then looked in the mirror again. I got out my gel and spiked my hair. I sighed.

"I look funny," I said to Kirk who was standing just behind me, watching me in the mirror.

"You always look funny," Jaden said from his bunk.

"Shut up, Jaden."

"You're just not used to having black hair. You look good," Kirk said.

"You're not just saying that?"

"Oh, stop obsessing over your hair!" yelled Jaden. "You look fine! Quit whining!"

"See?" Kirk said. "You know Jaden didn't say that to make you feel good."

That was true enough. I looked in the mirror again.

"I guess it doesn't look too bad," I said.

"It looks fine. Think of it as a makeover. You gay dudes are into that, right?" Kirk said.

"Oh, be quiet."

I couldn't help but smile.

"Let's go do something," Kirk said. "It's almost time for supper. We can shoot a few hoops."

"Are you crazy? I just showered. I'm not getting sweaty, and my people don't do basketball."

"You're just saying that because you know I'll kick your butt."

"As if! Come down to the wrestling mats sometime and I'll show you a butt kicking. You'll be begging for mercy."

"In your dreams, Lincoln."

"Yeah, you're scared."

"Scared of a little homo like you? I don't think so."

"Hey!" yelled Jaden.

"What?" I asked.

"Why do you go postal if I say something about you being gay, but Kirk can say anything he wants and you either don't care or think it's funny?"

"Because you called me a faggot, and he calls me stuff like gay and homo. When you said it, you were being nasty. There was hate behind it. When Kirk says stuff to me, he's being funny or giving me a hard time as a friend."

Jaden looked down at the floor for a moment.

"Listen, I'm sorry I called you that, okay? I just...I always thought...but you're not like I thought you'd be. You're like...normal."

I laughed.

"Did you expect me to wear a dress or something?" I asked.

"Well, yeah. I thought you were going to be all...what's the word...flashy or..."

"Flamboyant?" Kirk asked.

"Yeah, that's it. Flailing your hands around and talking with a lisp and being a big sissy."

"Well, I bet he would throw a hissy fit if I wrinkled his shirt right now," Kirk said, mischievously.

"Or punch you in the face," I said in my best smart-aleck tone.

"Like that," Jaden said. "I never expected you to punch me in the face, and Mr. Brubaker says you're an incredible wrestler. I didn't know you guys could be tough."

"Well, I don't know everyone who is gay, so I can't speak for all of us, but I'm just me. I don't really like sports, but I do like wrestling and fencing."

"Yeah, so. I'm sorry. I shouldn't have called you that name."

"Then, I'm sorry I punched you in the face."

"Awe, I think you guys should hug," Kirk said.

"Let's not get crazy," Jaden said.

"Great, you guys have talked so long that it's almost time for supper. Now we don't have time to do anything," Kirk said.

"Have you noticed how whiny Kirk is?" I asked Jaden.

"Yeah, now that you mention it, I have," Jaden said.

"Oh, shut up, both of you," Kirk said. He grunted. "I liked it better when you hated each other."

Jaden and I looked at each other and grinned.

Our cabin mates began to wander in, and each of them gawked at my hair. It made me uneasy. I looked at myself in the mirror again. I looked so weird with black hair.

Cody's table was full when we went down to the dining hall, but there was Elijah sitting and grinning at me. Now, I wasn't sorry at all I'd put *Icy Hot* in his briefs. I wished I could do it again, but Mr. Brubaker had confiscated my only jar. I'd brought it to camp thinking I probably wouldn't use it since it was kind of a doomsday weapon.

I don't think Cody noticed me, which was just as well. I hoped he didn't think I was weird for dying my hair. I could tell him the truth, but then I'd look like a whiner, and Cody might even think Elijah was cool for pulling off such a good practical joke. The truth would make me look stupid, too. I should have known something was wrong with my conditioner. I was such an idiot.

It was make-your-own-taco night, and the tacos and chips and salsa put me in a better mood. Besides, the dance was only a couple of hours away, and I was going to be with Cody! If Elijah thought I'd stay away because of my hair, he was sooo wrong! I wasn't giving up. Before the night was through, I was going to dance with Cody Studebaker in front on the whole camp!

I lingered at the table with Kirk and my cabin mates. Jaden was being a lot nicer, and I'd always gotten along well with Andy, Todd, and the others. We talked and ate and laughed. I loved the tacos, but I had to be really careful to keep from spilling anything on me. I'd decided I looked best in the royal-blue polo I was wearing, and I didn't want to have to change.

I got nervous as the time for the dance grew near. I walked down to the lake by myself. I wanted to be alone for a while. What if Cody didn't like my black hair? What if I said something stupid? What if he didn't like the way I danced?

I had to stop myself from thinking about everything that could go wrong. I was being stupid. I was usually a lot more confident, but this was a big night for me. Cody Studebaker was the cutest boy I'd ever met, and there was just something about him... I still couldn't believe he was gay! I felt as if I'd won the lottery when I'd found out. If only I could make Elijah disappear.

Cody already liked me. I needed to remember that. We were fencing buddies. We walked together after class, and sometimes he flirted with me. He even did it right in front of girls, so he wasn't trying to hide how he felt about me. Yeah, he liked Elijah, too, but the contest wasn't over. Cody was going to be mine.

I walked back up to the cabin feeling a lot better. My black hair threw me off, but mostly I was confident. I was also determined not to let Elijah's prank get to me.

The other guys were getting ready for the dance when I returned to the cabin. I caught Kirk holding up two shirts and looking back and forth between them.

"Now who can't make a decision?"

"Shut up and help me. You guys are supposed to be good at fashion, right?"

"That's one stereotype that's absolutely true," I said.

I ended up picking out clothes for just about all my cabin mates. Jaden actually came and asked if I would help him. We were getting along much better than before.

The minutes slipped by, and finally it was time to depart. I sprayed on come cologne and walked toward the dance with my cabin mates. I almost laughed at how they were clustered close together. Were heteros always so afraid of girls? I never had been, but then I had nothing to lose. I guess I was almost as bad. I was being bolder at camp, but if I hadn't known for sure that Cody was gay, I would have been far more cautious. I probably wouldn't have made a move... period. I didn't know how, and I doubted any hetero boy would react well to another boy hitting on him. It's too bad hetero boys couldn't just take the interest of a boy like me as a compliment, but then the world did have a lot of problems.

Kirk hung back when we arrived at the parking lot. All the cars were had been parked elsewhere, and the large, flat space had been turned into a big dance area surrounded by lights and speakers. Kirk gazed at Kayla with longing. I resisted the urge to make fun of him.

"Go on," I said. "You know she likes you. Go talk to her."

The DJ started in, and the music began playing. Kirk still hesitated. I looked over and spotted Cody. Elijah was already talking to him. I didn't have time to waste.

"Come on. Let's go over. I'll come with you."

I grabbed Kirk's arm and led him toward Kayla. Straight boys were so tragic.

Once I got him going, he walked on his own. By the time Kayla spotted us, there was no evidence I'd been dragging Kirk toward her.

"Hi, Kirk. Hi, Curtis."

"Hey," Kirk said.

"Kirk was right," I said. "He spotted you from across the dance, and he told me you look prettier than ever."

Kayla beamed, and Kirk blushed.

"Okay, I just wanted to say hi. I have my eye on a *very* cute boy," I said.

"Good luck," Kirk said.

"You're so nice and so supportive," Kayla said to Kirk as I walked away. I smiled.

I didn't hesitate as I walked toward Cody. I might have been as hesitant as Kirk if Cody had been alone, but since Elijah was already with him, I wanted to get in there as fast as possible. I might not have hesitated, anyway, because getting to Cody first would have been an advantage. I guess I'd never know.

"Wow, you aren't blond anymore!" Cody said as I approached.

"I thought I'd try something new," I said, giving Elijah a momentary stare.

"I like it," Cody said.

I grinned at Elijah. His ploy had failed.

"You want to dance?" I asked.

I couldn't believe I was bold enough to ask him so quickly, especially since a whole bunch of butterflies had taken flight in my stomach, but I went for it. I wanted to beat Elijah to it, and I wanted to ask before I lost my nerve.

"Uh... I don't know. We'll be the only two guys dancing together."

Cody looked around, suddenly nervous.

"Everyone already knows we're both gay," I said. "Most of them seem cool with it, and we can't let those who aren't stop us from having fun."

"I'm a little nervous about it," Cody said.

He wasn't just a little nervous. He was a *lot* nervous. He was actually trembling. I had no idea dancing in public would be so hard for him.

"How about if Elijah joins us? Then, we'll be three guys dancing together," I asked.

Cody looked more comfortable, but Elijah looked shocked. He probably wondered if I was up to something devious. I actually wasn't, for once. I really wanted to dance with Cody, and he looked so nervous I feared he'd hurl. I wanted to make things easier on him, and dancing with Cody and Elijah would be a lot better than not dancing with Cody at all.

Cody looked around for a few moments, and I was getting worried that he wouldn't dance with me, period.

"Yeah, okay," he said at last.

"Come on," I took him by the hand and led him into the small group of dancers that was slowly growing larger. Elijah came with us.

I began dancing, then Elijah joined in and, finally, Cody. Both boys were very good dancers. Cody had the moves of a natural athlete, and Elijah had great control over his muscled body. I was a great dancer, if I do say so myself.

Cody grinned and became more at ease as some girls began to dance near us. I wanted to dance one-on-one with Cody, just him and me, but he was a little less brave than I'd thought. Dancing in a group made him more comfortable, and if that's what it took, then it was better than not dancing with him at all.

I focused on Cody as we danced, staying as close to him as I could. He gazed into my eyes and smiled as girls closed in on him on either side. Elijah was right there, too, of course. The three of us formed a little triangle that became the center of the dance.

I pretended that Cody and I were dancing alone. It was just him and me. He was so good-looking and so...so everything that attracted me to another boy. I yearned to lean in and kiss him, but I didn't have the nerve to do it in front of so many people. My heart raced at the very thought, and I felt lightheaded but happy.

Our little group danced and laughed. Sometimes, even Elijah and I faced each other and danced for a few moments. He wasn't so bad, really. True, I now had black hair because of him but only as a result of our prank war. We were rivals for Cody's attention, not true enemies.

The girls were drawn to the three of us. Perhaps they felt comfortable with us because we were gay boys. We didn't play games with them and had no ulterior motives. We were boys and yet not quite the same as most boys.

I enjoyed being the center of attention. I had never felt so popular. Being gay was difficult sometimes, but I knew I was truly lucky to be one of the few. My uncle had told me it was a gift. I'd thought of it more as a curse most of the time, but maybe he was right after all.

We danced through several songs, then Cody, Elijah, and I headed toward the refreshment table as one. Some of the girls tagged along, laughing and talking to the three of us and especially to Cody. I didn't blame them. Cody was by far the cutest. He was the best-looking boy in the whole camp.

As we stood there drinking punch, I suddenly remembered the wristband I'd worked so hard to complete. I reached in my pocket and drew it out.

"I told you I'd finish it," I said to Cody as I handed it to him.

"It's awesome!"

Cody actually hugged me. I rolled my eyes with pleasure as his strong arms squeezed me tight. I could feel his heart beating in his chest. My own heart raced. Cody Studebaker hugged me!

I helped Cody put on the wristband. It looked so sexy on him. The girls loved it and even ran their hands up his arm. Cody grinned. He loved all the attention.

Cody looked at me nervously and grinned slightly. Time slowed, and the whole world moved in slow motion. Cody's eyes shifted to the girls for a moment, and then he leaned in and kissed me on the lips. Our kiss lasted only a few moments, but my heart soared. I had never been as happy as I was at that moment.

Cody grinned shyly as he pulled back. He pushed the hair out of his face. He was sooo cute. The girls whispered quietly among themselves. Elijah frowned and looked like he might even cry. The rumor of our kiss spread throughout the dance.

We soon returned to dancing. Cody grinned at me as we danced, but he smiled at Elijah a lot, too. He even sometimes focused his attention on Elijah as we danced. Elijah smiled, but sadly. I think he felt what I did, that Cody had chosen me. Yes!

I was happy enough to walk on air, but the sad look in Elijah's eyes made me pity him. I knew what it felt like to have a crush on a boy who didn't like me back. Cody did like Elijah, but not the way Elijah wanted him to like him. Even in my elated state I felt sorry for him.

The dance pulled Cody away from us, and I couldn't even get near him after a while. There were too many girls surrounding him. Elijah wandered off, and I danced with a few different girls. I enjoyed dancing with them, but I wanted to be with Cody.

I took a breather since I couldn't dance with Cody. I spotted Elijah over by the refreshment table. He looked more downcast than ever. He gazed at me sadly as I grabbed a bottle of water and joined him.

"I guess you won," he said.

There was no anger or hatred in his voice, only sadness.

"You know, Cody likes you, too."

"Yeah, we're friends, but I wanted to be more than friends. I wanted him to hug me like he hugged you. I wanted him to kiss me like..."

Tears welled up in Elijah's eyes, and a sob escaped despite his best efforts to hold it in. He turned and quickly walked away from the dance. I paused for a moment, unsure of what to do. I looked back at the dance. Cody was dancing in the middle of a crowd of girls. I looked at Elijah, quickly retreating into the darkness, and hurried after him.

Elijah sat on one of the huge boulders by the flagpoles. He looked down at the ground and tried not to cry. I sat close to him, but I didn't know what to say.

"No one ever wants me," he said quietly. "It's so hard. I get crushes on boys, but they never like me back."

A sob escaped from Elijah, and I put my hand on his shoulder.

"I met Cody, and he was just...wow. Then, when I found out he was actually gay, I couldn't believe it. Usually I fall for a boy only to find out he likes girls, but Cody...not only is he totally hot and sexy and nice, he's gay, too!"

"I know *exactly* what you mean," I said.

"But, once again, the boy I like doesn't like me back."

"He likes you."

"He doesn't like me the way I want him to like me. He doesn't like me the way he likes you."

"Um...sorry?" I said, shrugging my shoulders.

"I should hate you," Elijah said, "but you're too nice to hate."

"Even after I put *Icy Hot* in your underwear?"

"Yes, and after putting a rotting fish under my bed. That thing was nasty."

"Found that, did you? I wondered."

"It almost made me puke." Elijah laughed for a moment.

"Listen, I don't know why Cody *likes* me," I said. "I'll be completely honest. I was afraid he'd go for you. Okay, I was terrified you'd get him and I'd be left out."

"Yeah, hotties really go for short guys."

"You're not tall, but you're not short, and I'd trade my height for your muscles any day. What do you do, work out all the time? I'm skinny and pathetic compared to you."

Elijah smiled.

"You're making it really hard to hate you."

"It's all part of my devious plan."

"Stop making me laugh. You're ruining my pity party."

"I don't want you to be sad, Elijah. Despite the fact that you put dye in my hair conditioner, you're a great guy. That's what made me so afraid you'd get Cody, that and your awesome bod."

Elijah sighed.

"You really think I'll find someone?" Elijah asked.

"Are you kidding? If I hadn't been crushing on Cody so bad, and if we weren't spending all our spare time tormenting each other..."

I swallowed. Once again my mouth was running faster than my brain.

"What?" Elijah asked.

I could feel my face grow hot and red. I was glad it was mostly dark so Elijah couldn't see.

"Well...I was thinking that...we could have been boyfriends."

I looked away. I couldn't look in Elijah's eyes. He reached over, grasped my chin, and made me look at him.

"You mean that, don't you?"

"Yeah. I didn't mean to say it out loud, but I meant it."

"Thanks, Curtis."

We both stood up. After an awkward pause, Elijah hugged me. I held him in my arms and squeezed him tight. When we released each other, Elijah smiled.

"I guess you should go dance with your boyfriend," he said.

Elijah started to walk away, but I grabbed his hand.

"Come on, let's go dance. You don't want to be alone. Come have fun with the rest of us."

Elijah smiled and let me lead him back toward the dance.

"What was it like kissing Cody?" Elijah asked.

"Like Heaven on Earth, "I said.

"You do have it bad for him, maybe even more than me."

"He's all I can think about."

"I can't say I'm happy that you beat me out for him, but I am happy that you're happy."

"Come on, let's check out cute boys. We'll pick one out for you."

We rejoined the dance. Cody danced with us, but it was more like a big group dance, with everyone dancing with everyone else. At least, here people danced. Not much dancing went on at school dances. They shouldn't have been called dances at school at all. They shouldn't have been called "school stand-arounds."

I was hoping for another kiss, but it didn't happen. Cody flirted with me and sometimes looked as if he was about to move in and kiss me, but he didn't. The girls were eyeing the two of us, and I felt a little like I was living in a fish bowl. I liked the attention, and yet it was weird having girls watch what I did with another boy.

I made an effort to include Elijah, and Cody paid quite a bit of attention to him, too. I even got a little jealous now and then. I guess old habits die hard. I also couldn't believe that Cody picked me over Elijah!

Cody disappeared near the end of the dance, so I danced with Elijah and the girls. I was kind of going to miss our feud, but it was also nice not think of Elijah as the enemy.

I was sweaty from all the dancing, so when the dance ended, Elijah and I headed for the refreshment table, and I grabbed another bottle of water. We walked toward the cabins. The moon was shining bright overhead.

"Want to go for a short walk?" Elijah asked. "I don't feel like going back to my cabin yet."

"You aren't going to beat me up, are you?" I teased.

"I'm afraid you might get me down and pin me. I've heard about your legendary wrestling moves."

I laughed.

I followed Elijah as he turned and walked toward the crafts area.

"So, am I forgiven for all the rotten things I did to you?" I asked.

"Hmm, the *Icy Hot* really hurt!"

"Yeah, I felt guilty after I did it, but it seemed like a good idea at the time. You did get me back by sabotaging my hair."

"Ha ha! Yeah! I didn't know you'd still be cute with black hair. I was hoping you'd look bad if you weren't blond."

"We're both just a little bit evil, aren't we?"

"Yeah, but I forgive you."

"I forgive you, too."

"Listen, why did you get so upset when I ran your boxer-briefs up the flagpole? Someone told me you cried. I felt bad about that."

"It wasn't the underwear. It was the note. You see, my mom is dead, and when I saw that note...it just hit me wrong."

"Oh, I feel like such a jerk now."

"You didn't know. You didn't mean to be cruel."

"I wouldn't hurt anyone like that on purpose."

"I know that, Elijah. I knew it even then. That's why I didn't get mad at you. The underwear up the flagpole thing was a good joke."

"Sometimes the classics are best."

"Yeah."

We talked about the nasty tricks we'd pulled on each other and laughed about them. Elijah was in a much better mood than he had been.

We walked up into the Scouting area and almost tripped on a couple making out on the grass. I was about to say something to Elijah about the disgusting heterosexual display, but he was staring at the couple with his mouth hanging open.

"Cody?"

My jaw dropped open, too. There was Cody Studebaker, making out with...a girl!

"What the..."

Cody stood up quickly, wiping leaves and grass off his legs. A pretty blonde girl stood up awkwardly beside him.

"I'd better go," she said. "Bye, Cody."

"Bye."

I just stared at Cody Studebaker, trying to keep tears from welling up in my eyes.

"What's going on?" I asked, completely confused.

"I...uh...I..." Cody stammered. "Crap."

"Would you care to explain?" I asked.

"Well...you're going to be mad."

"I think you owe me an explanation. At the dance you made it pretty clear you were interested in me, and now here we find you—making out with a girl! What kind of gay boy are you?"

"Well, I'm not really...that is."

"Are you bi?" Elijah asked.

"No. I'm..."

"What?" I asked.

"I'm not gay."

"*What?*" Elijah and I both asked loudly, our voices rising higher than they probably had since we were nine.

"I was just pretending."

"Pretending? You were pretending to be gay?" I asked, incredulously.

"Well, I thought the girls would pay more attention to me if they thought I was gay. There's a gay boy at my school, and the girls are always hovering around him."

"You kissed me!"

"Well...all the girls were watching, and they knew that we...I kind of had to."

My world came crashing down. Tears welled up in my eyes.

"Do you even like me?" I asked, just barely keeping a sob from escaping. Elijah detected it. He looked at Cody with narrowed eyes.

"Yeah, I like you. I like you both. You're cool. I never hung out with gay guys before. I thought it would be creepy, but..."

"You've been lying to us the whole time!" Elijah said. "You've been letting us make fools of ourselves competing for your attention! I put dye in Curtis's hair conditioner, and he put Icy Hot in my underwear!"

Cody fought not to laugh. He knew it was not the time. He looked kind of scared. He was outnumbered two to one, after all.

"I think we should beat the crap out of him," Elijah said. "Maybe we should mess up his pretty face!"

I put my hand on Elijah's chest to hold him back. He was losing control.

"I never meant to make fools of you. I'm sorry. I just wanted the girls to pay attention to me."

"Why would you have to do anything to get them to pay attention to you? You're the best-looking guy in the whole camp!" I said.

"Girls are afraid to approach me sometimes. I thought that if they thought I was gay, they wouldn't be afraid."

"You used us!" I said.

"Well...I didn't mean to use you. I thought you'd like the attention I gave you, and...I did kiss you. I've never kissed a boy before."

"So all this was so you could make out with one girl?"

"Well...not just one."

"How many?"

"Six."

"Six! So... All these girls are laughing at Elijah and me because they know you're just using us?"

"No! No. They still think I'm gay."

"I'm totally confused," Elijah said.

"Well, you know girls...they want to fix things. They figure that if they make out with me, they can make me straight."

"We're not broken!" Elijah said. "There's nothing wrong with being gay, jerk!"

"No. Of course there's not, but girls see a gay boy as a challenge, right?"

He did have a point, but I wasn't going to admit it.

"I can't believe you used us," I said.

"I'm sorry."

"I think we should beat him up," Elijah repeated.

"We're not going to beat him up," I said. I turned to Cody. "I really thought you liked me."

"I do like you, just not...like that. I'll admit I flirted, and I led you both on. I didn't mean for you to find out. Camp is over tomorrow. I figured you'd go home and tell your friends about the hot blond boy you met this summer. Think about it. If you hadn't found out I'm not gay, you'd be excited about what happened at the dance, Curtis. And, Elijah, I know I hurt you, and I didn't mean to, but I was going to talk to you tomorrow and tell you we could still be friends. I was going to write you over the winter."

"Great! I spend my whole time at camp running after a straight boy!" I said.

"Well, you both got something out of it you're overlooking," Cody said.

"What?" I asked.

"You probably wouldn't have met each other if you both hadn't been chasing me. By the way, I think you two would make a good couple."

Elijah and I looked at each other. Cody was right. We probably wouldn't have met if it weren't for him.

"Besides, you got to hang out with a hot straight boy," Cody said with mock conceit – at least I think it was mock and not the real thing.

I looked at Elijah.

"Now I think we should beat him up."

"Okay! Okay! I am sorry guys. I didn't mean to hurt either one of you. I really like you both. Forgive me? Please?"

Cody looked back and forth between us with puppy-dog eyes.

"Please?"

"Okay! I forgive you!" I said.

Cody looked at Elijah, who wasn't talking.

"I think I owe you something," Cody said. He leaned in and kissed Elijah on the lips. I thought Elijah was going to pass out. "There, you guys are even now. You both got to kiss me."

"Wow," Elijah said, looking at me after he recovered. "What an ego. He doesn't even kiss that well."

"I do, too!"

"Yeah, right, straight boy. You hetero guys can't kiss. Really, Curtis, you should have told me he was a lousy kisser. How could you not know he's straight after a crummy kiss like that?"

I grinned. I knew Elijah was putting Cody on.

"I didn't think it was polite. I guess it should have tipped me off that he isn't gay. No gay boy would be that bad at kissing."

"I'm not bad at kissing!"

Elijah patted Cody on the back.

"Of course, you're not," Elijah said.

"Oh, shut up!" Cody said.

"By the way, I forgive you, too," Elijah said.

Elijah and I walked back toward camp with Cody following.

"He really does need work on his kissing," Elijah said to me.

"I'm right here! I can hear you!"

"Can you imagine being so pathetic you pretend to be gay to get girls?" I said. "I knew straight guys were desperate, but really," I said.

"I hate you guys!" Cody said.

"Shut up or we'll un-out you," Elijah said.

"Yeah, we'll tell the whole camp you're not gay."

"You guys are just evil," Cody said.

"I think our work here is done," Elijah said.

"Oh, no, it's just beginning. I have some dirty tricks I didn't get to use on you. What do you think we should do to Cody first?"

"You guys are scaring me," Cody said.

"Be afraid, be very afraid," I said. "Always beware the wrath of the gay boys."

"Great, now I won't be able to sleep tonight," Cody said.

"We won't do anything to you—probably," I said.

"You still have that jar of *Icy Hot*?" Elijah asked.

"I'll see if I can sneak it out of my counselor's room."

"Guys! Come on!"

"Have we tormented him enough?" I asked.

"Yeah, but there's always next year," Elijah said.

"And maybe tonight," I added.

Elijah smiled at me and took my hand. We giggled as Cody hurried along behind us begging us not to prank him in his sleep. Sometimes, even straight boys can be fun.

***

We didn't do anything nasty to Cody that night. As long as he was with us, we pretended we might, but as soon as he was gone, Elijah and I had a good laugh about it.

"You think we made him think he's a lousy kisser?" Elijah asked.

"I think he knows he's good, but it was fun to play with his head, and he does deserve it."

"I never suspected for a moment that he wasn't gay!" Elijah said.

"I didn't, either."

"We must have lousy gaydar," Elijah said.

"No. We just didn't stop to think that he might be lying. What hetero boy would lie and claim to be gay?"

Elijah and I looked at each other and grinned.

"Cody!" we both said simultaneously.

"I feel kind of like a fool, but two good things did come out of this," I said.

"Yeah?"

"We both got to kiss Cody. I bet we are the only boys who will *ever* get to kiss him."

"My head was spinning. He's so hot!"

"Down, Elijah. Remember, he's not gay."

"Yeah, so what is the other thing?"

"We each gained a new friend."

Elijah smiled.

"Maybe next summer we can be more than friends."

I grinned back. I leaned in and kissed Elijah. I had the feeling our kiss was the start of something big.

Books by Mark A. Roeder

Note: The books below are meant for older readers and contain material that may not be suitable for younger readers.

Listed in suggested reading order

Outfield Menace

Snow Angel

The Soccer Field Is Empty

Someone Is Watching

A Better Place

The Summer of My Discontent

Disastrous Dates & Dream Boys

Just Making Out

Temptation University

The Picture of Dorian Gay

Someone Is Killing The Gay Boys of Verona

Vampire's Heart

Keeper of Secrets

Do You Know That I Love You

Masked Destiny

Altered Realities
Dead Het Boys
This Time Around
Phantom World
Second Star to the Right
The Perfect Boy
The Graymoor Mansion Bed and Breakfast
Shadows of Darkness
Heart of Graymoor
Yesterday's Tomorrow
Boy Trouble
Christmas In Graymoor Mansion

Also by Mark A. Roeder

*Homo for the Holidays: A Collection of
Mostly Gay Christmas Tales*

CPSIA information can be obtained
at www.ICGtesting.com
Printed in the USA
LVOW10s0836260217
525454LV00001B/142/P